PINK SLIME

H.E. GOODHUE

FOR ALL THE CARNIVORES I KNOW AND LOVE

Pink Slime

Two curved neon lines salaciously lit up the night sky like the kind of yellowed, nicotine stained smile only found on dimly lit street corners supported by two bruised legs wrapped in torn fishnets. At least that was how Andy Holstein felt as he parked his dented, two-door vintage shitbox classic in the jaundiced glow of the fast food restaurant's sign. The car groaned and then released a metallic sigh of relief as Andy hefted his considerable girth from the driver's seat. He paused before shutting the door. The car was beginning to lean to the left. Andy sadly shook his head and slammed the door.

The sign called to him, its beautiful glow drawing him in like a moth to a porch light. Andy had sworn to himself that he would drive directly home after work today. He would just continue past the restaurant without stopping. There would be no trip through the drive-thru today. No second gastronomic vacation to his honorary seat near the ball pit. Andy was going to go right home after work today.

WAS going to…but then, Andy's day went to shit. In all honesty, this day hadn't really gone that much worse than any other. Every day for a comically oversized running shoe salesman was pretty much terrible. Selling something that you clearly don't use was simply more irony than minimum wage should buy.

Yeah, Andy wore sneakers, but he sure as hell didn't go jogging in them. No, Andy's feet had swollen beyond the confines of regular shoes, leaving triple wide sneakers as his only option. That was how Andy first found himself inside an athletic supply store, let alone one named "Jim's Rockin' Pitch." The owner, Jim, had named the store in honor of himself and his life altering accomplishment - shattering the state's pitching record in high school. Since then, Jim hadn't broken much beyond his knuckles and a few marriages. He also hadn't bothered to replace the bulbs as they died in the store's sign out, instead choosing to allow it to read "J___ock__ Itch".

For some reason, Jim offered Andy a job. Maybe it was some sort of weight related affirmative action or maybe he thought it would be funny to have a fat guy selling running shoes in a sporting goods store. Either way, Andy had no other options, so he took the ten percent employee discount on his triple wide shoes and the job.

Since then, all the other salesmen at Jock Itch, their chests puffed out in a show of muscled bravado, undersized referee shirts stretched thin, made it a point to ruin just about every day that Andy didn't call in sick. And he couldn't even do that anymore. He had used all his sick days and Jim was going to fire him if he missed another day.

But today had been worse. Today, Cece Adams had come in to buy a new sports bra. Andy didn't see her come in. If he had, he would have hidden in the stock room, silently watching the lithe blonde haired beauty that was Cece Adams. Andy had secretly nurtured a crush on Cece since grade school. Now he felt like he would be more likely just to crush her.

Todd, head salesman and president of the 'I can bench more pounds than I have brain cells' club, called Andy up the register after Cece had wandered into the back of the store. The minute Todd introduced himself as, "Todd, the D's are doubled cuz that's how I like 'em," Andy knew that he was in trouble. Todd was nineteen, same as Andy, but that was where the similarities ceased.

"What's up, Candy Andy?" Todd smirked.

"I dunno," Andy shrugged. "You called me up here. Shouldn't I be asking that question?"

"Huh?" Todd asked, momentarily confused. "Yeah, no wait…shut the hell up!"

"Okay," Andy shrugged and began shuffling back to his spot in the badminton aisle.

"Hey, Candy Andy," Todd shouted, "I didn't call you up here to scope out your tig ol' bitties. There's some merch left in changing room 5. Some a-hole kid left it locked, so pop the handle and reshelf the merch."

Cece was midway through trying on her new sports bra when Andy popped the lock and lumbered into the dressing room. She paused, hands in the air, completely exposed and unsure of what to do.

"Oh!" Andy cried as he stumbled backwards and fell to the floor. "Oh! Cece oh!" He couldn't find any other words and immediately regretted the few he had uttered. His legs, thick as tree trunks, flailed helplessly before a loud *rip* stopped his movement. Andy had torn the seam in his cheap black polyester pants.

Cece opted for high-pitched screaming. The other salesman came running in as Cece slammed the door.

"Andy, you pervert!" Todd shouted. "How many times do we need to tell you this ain't no peep show?" The other salesmen laughed, congratulating Todd on his joke.

"Go away!" Cece screamed. "Go away right now or I'm calling the cops!"

Todd led the other boys away as Andy scrambled up from the floor. He could feel the cool breeze sneaking through the tear and dancing across his tighty-whities. Cece's screams followed Andy into the stock room where he desperately searched for a roll of duct tape to fix his pants.

Normally, there were countless rolls of every color and pattern imaginable, but Jim must have forgotten to order more and the only roll Andy could find was one with tiny yellow rubber ducks peppering a powdery pink background. Andy groaned as he taped his pants back together and willed the day to go faster.

So yes, Andy had promised his older sister Rachel that he wouldn't stop for fast food. That he would attempt to join her in her newest health craze. He had promised that he would come home and at least try some roasted vegetables and seaweed, but that had been before Todd, before Cece, and before the ducks.

"The ducks!" Andy hissed as he stood in line, his hand involuntarily pawing at his butt. The intoxicating aroma of French fries had momentarily blunted Andy's painful memories and left him blind to the fact that he currently had a wide stripe of pink tape with yellow ducks creeping up his butt crack. He could hear children snickering behind him in line. "God, like it matters now? Like my day could possibly get any worse?"

"Um, hi, Andy," the cashier said, but the voice was different, lighter and sweeter than the usual one. Sure, they all knew Andy by name. How could they not, with two to three daily visits, but this voice was both new and completely known.

"Oh crap, it's you!" Andy exclaimed as he stared at Cece behind the counter, a triangular paper hat perched perfectly upon her golden head.

"Don't you think I should be the one to say that after today?" Cece grinned, but her words were playful. "I mean, I'm the one who had someone bust into her changing room while they tried on clothes. Remember?"

Andy most definitely remembered. He would be sure to remember what Cece looked like for the rest of his life.

"I didn't do that on purpose," Andy explained. "I thought that, well, Todd said that there were clothes left in there."

"Todd is a total dildo," Cece smirked. "I knew you didn't do anything on purpose."

"Cece!" the manager called. "We only pay you to talk while talking orders. You can work on your personal life on your own time!"

Cece flushed, her face matching one of the colors adorning her triangular hat. "Jeez," she muttered. "Anyway, what'll you have, Andy?"

Hesitation swelled in Andy's chest. Should he order with some control? Should he really get what he wanted when Cece was the one taking his order? She would be disgusted by his request. *She probably IS already disgusted with you!* Andy's inner voice scorned. It didn't matter.

"I'll have the quadruple bacon cheeseburger," Andy's breath became short. He was excited by the prospect of such an incredible meal. "I'll also have a large fry and large diet cola."

"Value sized?" Cece asked without a note of ridicule.

"Yeah," Andy muttered as he fished the money from his pocket. He had long ago memorized the price of this meal.

"Number eight," Cece smiled as she handed Andy his receipt. "Should be up in a few."

"Thanks," Andy turned to walk away. "Sorry about today."

"No problem," Cece grinned. "Oh hey, Andy, one more thing."

"Yeah?" Andy asked, wondering if they had recently raised the price of his habitual bad day meal.

"Cute ducks!" Cece beamed, but again her words were light and playful, not meant to be hurtful.

"Quack, quack." Andy smiled sheepishly and grabbed his sack of food.

Andy walked slowly towards his table near the ball pit. He knew people were looking at him, at his ducks and laughing, but this was nothing new.

People had laughed at Andy his entire life. Laughed when his father abandoned his mother for local celebrity Sissy Circles, a midget stripper with a clubfoot and odd dance routine. Laughed when Andy's mother began overfeeding him as a means to ensure that he would never leave her as well. And laughed when she hung herself with a pair of Andy's oversized underwear. After that, Andy kept right on eating. Laughter was the soundtrack to Andy's life. He was just never the one who was laughing.

Andy's table was empty, it usually was. No one officially recognized this table as Andy's, but after the ball pit had been installed, the table was left oddly isolated from the others. No other customers wanted to appear strange or mildly pedophilic, sitting alone near the edge of a pit filled with screaming children and multi-colored plastic balls. These unspoken social stereotypes coupled with the pungent tang of stale urine ensured that Andy's table was always open. All of these reasons, especially the reek of old pee, weren't lost on Andy, but people already found him odd and the image of him sitting alone eating a quadruple bacon cheeseburger next to a pit of rainbow colored plastic balls did little to dispel any of those thoughts.

The upper third of Andy's gut lopped onto the top of the table, while the remaining two thirds spilled out like bread dough underneath. Andy shifted and tried to make himself more comfortable. This was a dance he did every time he ate here, but with the bench securely attached to the table, there was little Andy could do. Why would a fast food restaurant create tables that were clearly made for underfed twelve year olds, Andy wondered? Didn't they know the physical demands of their clientele? The image of a reclining bench and moveable table flashed through Andy's mind as he took his first bite. That would make sense, something that could be moved to accommodate the unique corpulent proportions of their customer base. After a few more thoughtful bites, Andy's mind went blessedly blank, a sense of something, not quite happiness, settling over him with each chew.

That feeling, the best one Andy had felt all day, began to wither and die as he watched Abraham "Squirrel" Moscovitz pass through the fingerprint-stained double glass doors. Andy tried to chew quicker and to return to his happy place, but it was no use. Squirrel was heading right towards him.

-2-

An unseen metallic object, no bigger than a bathtub, finished its second orbit of Earth. The exterior glistened like quicksilver under the shine of countless stars. Suddenly the object stopped, a small liquid ripple passing over it as its ends pulled inward, giving the object a perfectly round shape. After hanging motionless for a few moments, the object began to spin, gaining speed with each rotation. The sphere tapered downwards, forming a wicked looking point. The silvery exterior wavered as it transformed from an icy gray to a glowing orange, radiating waves of intense heat.

The object, now glowing a fiery red, dropped from where it spun above the Earth. Passing through the Earth's atmosphere, the object gained in both temperature and speed. Cutting through clouds, the object left a swath of lightning and thunder in its wake. Finding a suitable cloud, large and gray, the object came to halt with a thunderous clap.

Below, people remarked at the amazing ferocity of this unexpected summer storm. The thunder cracked with ear splitting intensity, especially the final clap. Some would jest that it sounded like a sonic boom, but never having heard one, had no idea how right they were.

The object, invisible to radar and hidden in the clouds, shuddered. Massive waves undulated across its surface as it resumed its original oblong shape. Something inside the object shifted, awakening from a long slumber. It had traveled across unknown galaxies and cosmos at speeds incomprehensible to the human mind to reach Earth. It had arrived.

-3-

Abraham Moscovitz was known to most as "Squirrel" because of his erratic chattering speech, small stature and bulging eyes. His parents, owners of the local health food store, were rightfully concerned about their son's ADHD. But true to their neo-hippy roots, Abraham's parents explored every possible holistic means of treating their overactive boy. They had tried. And tried. And failed.

Eventually, Abraham's parents had secretly tried a few medications with the same results as wheatgrass, gluten-free pasta and heavy metal blood detoxifications. Out of options, Abraham's parents had decided to learn to live with their son's hyperactivity and, like everyone else in town, began calling him "Squirrel".

Squirrel, the child of two granola-pushing flower children in a town full of corn-fed farm folk, had few options for friends. He was so bad at sports that he was fairly certain it was an actual disability. His parents said not to worry because organized sports were 'fascist' and 'only served to brainwash kids for the military' so even if Squirrel had wanted to play, he never would have been allowed to. With no other options and a weird nickname, Squirrel's isolation had led him to the only person in town who might be worse off than he was – Andy Holstein.

Looking for Andy involved going to one of three places – his house, the Jock Itch or checking the side of the ball pit. Finding Andy meant taking in a lungful of stale urine and grease-laden air. Andy was always there, always eating.

"Hey Andy," Squirrel grinned as he skittered across the restaurant and slid into the opposite bench.

Andy noticed that Squirrel faced none of the physical discomforts he had, but tried to ignore them and enjoy the company. Having company wasn't bad. It was the fact that the company was Squirrel that made it terrible. Andy could see the jittery boy getting ready to chatter incessantly, his words no doubt colored by his parents' indoctrination.

"Hi Squirrel," Andy grunted as he tore another mouthful from his burger. He hoped that he could chew loudly enough to drown out the other boy.

8

"You know that stuff is going to kill you," Squirrel began. "That stuff is like poison. You would probably be better eating poison, Andy. At least then you'd know what's in it. The government doesn't let companies lie about what kills rats, man, but it turns a blind eye to what goes into food. Doesn't it freak you out that you bought that whole meal for less than six bucks? Man, you couldn't buy a pound and a half of apples for that."

Andy sighed. This was how Squirrel usually started when he was going to go for a while.

"Theoretically, everything is killing us," Andy shrugged as he forced a fistful of fries into his mouth. "Even doing nothing. By doing nothing, you're technically killing yourself, right? So all that meditating that your parents do is really nothing more than a drawn out version of suicide. And you're right about the apples. You definitely couldn't buy any of your parents bruised up, mealy organic apples for less than six bucks." Andy smiled slightly. He had been saving that one for a time when he needed it.

Squirrel thought for a second, remaining uncharacteristically silent. Andy could actually see the small waves of antsy energy dancing across his friend's face.

"Whatever, Andy," Squirrel dismissed, "at least it's their choice, man. You're so addicted to the salt and fat and chemicals that you're not even really in control anymore, man. The government and food companies put stuff in there to keep you eating it. There should, like, be rehab for people strung out on extra value meals, man. Mary Jane isn't the problem, that's like medicine. It's hamburgers and chicken nuggets that are destroying this country. That's the new crack. Shit, both were made by the government anyway."

"Put stuff in here?" Andy scoffed as he thrust his half-eaten bacon cheeseburger at Squirrel. "You're such a green weenie, man. There's nothing in here but beef."

"Beef?" Squirrel laughed. "Andy they can grind up buttholes and lips and it still counts as beef. That word only means it's part of a cow, but doesn't mean what part. You have no idea what you're putting into your body right now. There could be slime in there, man. You could be eating slime right now."

"Slime?" Andy paused. This was a new angle for Squirrel. "What the hell are you talking about, slime? This burger is solid." Andy poked the patty with his thick finger.

"That's the beauty of pink slime, Andy," Squirrel nodded. "The government lets meat companies cut ground beef with it. Think about it. You buy meat that's eighty percent ground beef, right? Man, what the heck do you think the other twenty percent is? I'll tell you, it's fat and pink slime."

"Now it's *pink* slime?" Andy mocked. "I was worried before, but now that I now that it's pink slime, well, now I'm terrified." Andy tore another hunk of meat from his towering cheeseburger.

"Dude, it's in there," Squirrel stated emphatically. "They take all the leftover bits of garbage beef and spin that stuff in a machine with like ammonia gas or something. The proteins liquefy and run out where they collect it and mix it into ground beef to bulk it up. Think about it, Andy. That whole process is totally crazy. Where the hell would someone even think that up? It should be science fiction, not food. Man, that's what pink slime is...science fiction, like Soylent Green. That's what you're putting into your body right now."

Andy thought for a second, a wad of half chewed meat in his mouth. What Squirrel had just said sounded gross enough and it was probably true, but it's not like the government would allow people to eat something that wasn't safe. And in the end who cares? Pink slime, whatever the hell it was, tasted damn good.

"Whatever, Squirrel," Andy mumbled as he resumed his chewing. "It's not like they would let us eat something that wasn't safe."

Squirrel tried to contain his acerbic laughter and failed miserably. It came out as a strange chortling cough that caught the attention of a mother of two at the nearest table, who then shoveled the remainder of her children's meals into greasy paper bags festooned with the latest cartoon characters. The kids began having tantrums almost immediately.

"I thought you were supposed to be happy when you ate those?" Squirrel shrugged and then turned back to Andy. "But, dude, that's crazy that you'd trust the corporations and government with your food. Pink slime wasn't even meant for people. In the

90s it was only allowed in dog food, but then all of a sudden, it's like totally safe for people to eat. Man, Canada doesn't even allow that stuff. It's illegal in Canada."

"Don't start with your Canadian Paradise speech," Andy warned. "I've heard that enough already. Everyone one knows that Canada is freaking wonderful, thank you very much, Squirrel. Canada does *everything* right, even the outlawing of the evil pink slime."

"Well, they do," Squirrel added sourly. "But whatever, Andy. Keep eating your toxic dog food. I don't even want to imagine how much of that crap you've filled your body with."

"Too much for it to matter now," Andy said, a note of sadness tingeing his words.

"Hey, whatever, right?" Squirrel chattered. "Sorry, Andy. It's your body, do what feels right."

"Yeah," Andy sighed, "it's my body." Andy glanced down where pockets of flesh bulged and lopped from his torso. He couldn't help but picture a trash bag filled with Jell-O. Pink Jell-O, if Squirrel was right.

Squirrel could see that he had gone too far. Sometimes, ADHD and politics did not lend themselves to being sensitive to your friend's needs.

"You want to go get stoned and play Xbox?" Squirrel asked, already knowing the answer.

"First intelligent thing you've said all night," Andy grinned and began pushing his trash onto the thick plastic tray in front of him.

As the two boys pushed open the doors and walked out into the parking lot, Squirrel stopped and stared up at the night sky.

"You see that?" he asked peering at a large cloud.

"See what? Is the government satellite that monitors your thoughts up there?" Andy mocked, as he opened the driver's side door.

"Seriously," Squirrel insisted, pointing at the edge of the cloud. "There's like a little shiny thing right there."

Andy looked where his friend pointed. Some small thing glinted faintly behind the cloud. "Dude, it's probably a plane or something."

"I dunno," Squirrel worried as he slipped into the car, his eyes locked on the cloud the entire time. "Planes would be moving. That thing isn't moving."

"Probably so far away that it looks like it's not moving," Andy offered. "Trick of the eye or something."

-4-

The cloud shifted. That was unforeseen and the object was left momentarily exposed. Sensors sounded, indicating that a human had made visual contact. The object darted behind the cloud and waited for the humans to move on to something else. It knew that humans had a long history of being unpredictable - evidently clouds were the same. The object would need to be more careful.

A series of ripples passed over object. The quicksilver coating had been ideal for space and passing through Earth's atmosphere, but it now caught errant beams of moonlight, making it periodically visible to more keenly aware human. The metallic outer shell became mirrored, appearing almost invisible as it reflected its surroundings. The passenger appraised the new cloaking pattern. This would be more suited for lower orbits where humans might be looking skyward.

With fear of detection no longer a concern, the passenger refocused on its true purpose. A test subject would need to be found. This area had many.

The object accelerated and was miles away in seconds. The upper crowns of trees shifted as the object silently rocketed past. Humans thought it was nothing more than a passing strong wind.

Finding a suitable subject and area from which to harvest it, the object came to a hovering stop above a large field. Running a quick scan of the surrounding area, the passenger determined that it was safe to collect a test subject.

Expanding into a large triangular shape, the object prepared to harvest the unsuspecting subject. A brilliant blue light shone from the center of the now triangular object. The test subject looked about, unsure of why it felt strange, but oddly at peace. As its feet were lifted off the ground, the test subject remained calm, as if completely unaware of the fact that it was now twenty feet above the ground on which it had once stood.

A ten-foot wide circle opened in the center of the object like the great beak of a giant mechanical squid. The subject showed no fear. Once the subject was securely inside, the opening disappeared, leaving behind no trace or seam of where it had once been.

The subject was kept calm by the ever-present shine of the blue light. It had no idea that the passenger was performing a series of surgical procedures and tests. Felt nothing as organs were removed, examined and replaced. The passenger ensured that the subject felt no discomfort as its blood was taken out, analyzed and determined to be problematic. Traces of the blight were present in the subject's system. This was only possible if it had been fed members of its own kind, which meant there would undoubtedly be a high degree of bioaccumulation. The passenger could not allow this subject to enter the food supply.

The bright blue light shone on the subject's head, keeping it docile and in a state free of pain, but a searing red light now shone on its body. The blood and muscle within the test subject was heated and dissolved in thin tendrils of smoke and steam that twisted from the subject's pores. Still it felt no pain. The subject had been sterilized and no longer posed a threat. The passenger did not enjoy performing this duty, but knew it must be done. Rules had been broken. Consequences followed. It was that simple.

The subject, now little more than withered skin and bone, passed back through the circle and was gently placed on the ground. It would have been preferable to dispose of the remains in another, somewhat more respectful way, but time did not allow.

The object shifted and resumed its oblong shape, appearing as little more than wrinkles in the night sky. Seconds later, the object was gone, returning to its previous post.

A desiccated corpse lay amidst the other cows like a deflated hide balloon. The other cows mooed plaintively, remaining blissfully unaware that their herd had just decreased by one.

-5-

A group of Marines moved with tight precision through the desolate city street. Their guns were raised and ready to deal with any unseen threats. Somewhere in the distance, a shadow moved across a rooftop. The men froze, waiting for their squad leader to give the next command. Should they engage and risk giving away their position or recon for more intel?

The squad leader motioned his decision. They would engage. After all, they were Marines and fortune favored the bold. A hail of gunfire erupted from the roof of the building at the end of the street. Tracer rounds lit up the night like hellish fireflies. The Marines ducked behind abandoned cars, returning fire and trying to keep from getting shot. Rounds pinged off the sidewalk, throwing chunks of concrete high into the air.

"GO! GO! GO!" the squad leader screamed as he tucked his head and ran towards the enemy. His men, well trained and fearless, followed close behind laying down cover fire as they ran.

A RPG round spiraled off the rooftop leaving a drunken corkscrew of smoke in its wake. The squad leader advanced, unaware of the impending danger that currently whizzed towards him and his men.

The explosion filled the street, as charred body parts pin-wheeled through the air, raining down on the screaming men who crawled through the bloody street.

-GAME OVER-

The words filled Andy's half of the split screen and then bled down to the bottom and pooled. Images of his soldiers writhed in the blood. He threw his controller down and grabbed a handful of chocolate covered Skittles, a treat of his own creation.

"Damn it, Squirrel," Andy growled as sugary strings stretched between his teeth. "Where the hell did you get a freaking RPG?"

"I found it," Squirrel shrugged as he looked over the stats from the round. He was slowly gaining on Andy.

"Found it?" Andy seethed. "You don't just find the damn RPG! Are you using a cheat? You must be using a cheat!"

"You've smoked too much, man," Squirrel laughed. "It's making you paranoid. Well, that and probably those candies. You know what high fructose corn syrup does your hormones?"

"Shut up, Squirrel," Andy snorted. He laughed a lot when he and Squirrel hung out in the basement playing Xbox. "Come on, I want a rematch."

Squirrel grabbed his controller. The times in the basement with Andy were some of the only ones where he could control the constant need to chatter. Maybe it was the videogames. Maybe it was something else.

"Andy! Andy, answer me right now!" Rachel shouted from the top of the basement stairs. "I can smell that crap all the way up to my room."

"Sorry," Andy coughed as a large cloud of smoke spilled from his mouth. "Squirrel tried washing them, but his underwear just has too many skid marks. I know the smell is bad."

"Gee, thanks," Squirrel smirked and then yelled up the stairs, "FYI, I'm commando! Just thought you might want to know, Rachel!"

"How appropriate," Andy smiled and then turned his attention back to his sister. "Don't worry, Rachel, Squirrel says he's not wearing any drawers, so the smell must just be your attitude."

Rachel sighed. It wasn't easy being both a sister and a guardian. Andy was so broken after their mother's suicide, so angry and Rachel had no idea how to bring her brother back. He was committing slow suicide with fast food and now he was experimenting with drugs too.

"Andy," Rachel said, the anger drained from her voice, "the least you could do is open a window. And did you try any of the roasted vegetables? It didn't look like you ate any. I swear, Andy, if I find out that you were back at that fast food place, I'm going to burn it down."

"Where do you keep the matches?" Squirrel shouted.

"Damn it, Andy," Rachel said. Her head *thunked* against the doorjamb. "Couldn't you even try? Couldn't you just not go there for one day, for me?"

"Get off my case," Andy said dismissively. "I had a long day. Why do you get so bent out of shape over where I have dinner? Shouldn't you be out on a date or something?"

The truth was that Rachel had given up on dating and any other semblance of a normal life once she became responsible for Andy. He was nineteen, but still a child, having been stunted by his parents' insane behavior.

"You just...I mean, that I just," Rachel paused. What she couldn't say was that she couldn't handle losing the only remaining family member that she had. She didn't think she could survive burying another family member, especially not under cheeseburger-related circumstances. "I don't know, Andy. I just do, okay? So sue me."

"Wouldn't be worth it," Andy teased. "I already know what you're worth." Andy tried his hardest to ignore the notes of sadness that hung on Rachel's words and cut into his heart.

"Yeah, okay, whatever," Rachel sighed. "Just open a damn window."

Squirrel jumped out of his chair and scampered towards the stairs.

"Where the hell are you going?" Andy shouted. "We're in the middle of a game."

"I heard something about roasted vegetables," Squirrel called over his shoulder as he continued up the stairs.

Andy took the game off pause and shot his friend's soldiers. He still felt like crap. Why did Rachel have to make his day even worse? Why couldn't she just accept things the way they were?

Loud banging in the kitchen signaled that Squirrel's vegetable quest had been fruitful. Andy listened to him microwave the food Rachel had worked hard to prepare for him, food he hadn't eaten. The pain in his heart flared.

Three winning rounds and eight fistfuls of chocolate covered Skittles later and Andy had forgotten the entire conversation.

-6-

The object hovered above a small gathering of the primitive dwellings. It scanned the life forms within, looking for traces of the blight. Most of them had it in their systems. How had they managed to ingest such large amounts of the blight?

As the passenger pondered this question and what would be the most prudent course of action, a smaller life form exited from one of the dwellings. It walked in slow clumsy steps. It was also alone. The passenger was there to observe and study. It was there to gather information, not to interact. It was allowed to examine some of the simpler life forms, but there remained no further information to gain from bovine test subjects. The passenger was hesitant to deviate from protocol. Was it being on Earth that was causing it to think of such things? Maybe these life forms, these humans, had some degree of a corrupting influence. Regardless of the consequences, the passenger made its decision. It had come with a task and it could not be accomplished without a human subject. There was no other choice.

The human continued its erratic path, starting and stopping without reason. At one point, the human stopped to sit and laugh, but there appeared to be no reason for such behavior.

Perhaps, this wasn't the best test subject, the passenger wondered, but time was of the essence. The blight had spread pervasively through multiple life forms. Furthermore, this subject was isolated and its extraction would not be noticed.

Glassy ripples spread from the center of the object, growing larger as they neared the edges. Its oblong shape stretched and became more defined as it resumed its triangular form. The mechanical beak-like port in the center opened and prepared to obtain the subject.

The human had no awareness of what was occurring above its head. The object was nearly invisible, but the blue light was not. A moment of panic spread over the subject, but was quickly erased by the blue light. The passenger prepared a table for the subject. It was larger than what was needed, being that it was typically used for bovine subjects, but it would work just the same. The previous bovine subject had not faired well. Perhaps the human one would do better.

-7-

Squirrel stumbled out of Andy's house. It was a little after two and he needed to get home. His parents never imposed a curfew, because that would be totalitarian, but they did draw the line with Squirrel sleeping at Andy's house. Squirrel always thought his parents' line the in sand about sleeping at Andy's was weird, but figured it had something to do with a fear of Andy being a bad influence. Squirrel smirked, thinking about his parents' concerns. Most parents worried that their teen's friends would get them into drinking, sex and drugs. Squirrel's parents, on the other hand, were kept up at night by fears of someone offering their son a cheeseburger or box of chicken nuggets.

Andy was the living embodiment of these fears, which was why Squirrel currently found himself zigzagging down the middle of the street with eyes as red as the communist flag his dad displayed proudly, in the basement, of course.

Squirrel's head felt strange. Not the strange it was supposed to feel like either. The hairs on the back of his neck were on end as if someone had snuck up behind him and was about to pounce. Squirrel spun to look behind him and almost tripped over his own feet.

"Ohhh, easy boy," Squirrel laughed as he steadied himself. He was relieved to see that the only thing that was behind him was an empty street. "Jeez, I must have smoked more than I thought. That or Dad has really outdone himself with this crop." Squirrel laughed again and continued towards his house, but couldn't shake the feeling that someone was watching him.

Something tickled the back of Squirrel's neck. It felt like little more than a gentle breeze, but it sent an icy chill shooting down his spine. His buzz suddenly began to wane as fear crept in. Squirrel could feel it – someone or something was watching him.

After a quick spinning circle, Squirrel still had yet to find who or what was watching him. He tried to quicken his pace. Tried to get home, but couldn't shake the feeling. A tiny voice in Squirrel's head shouted at him, screamed for him to look up. Squirrel stumbled to a stop and slowly, ever so slowly, raised his eyes towards the sky.

A section of the night sky seemed to ripple or move. The silken sheet of the starry above wrinkled and then snapped taut once again, but something was off. Some of the stars appeared to be placed at strange angles and were rapidly vibrating. Squirrel followed this series of oddly placed stars. They appeared further apart in one section, but slowly coming closer and closer, almost to a point. The pattern was near invisible with each tiny section vibrating at insane speeds. The motion should have rendered the abnormality invisible to the average human eye, but as was widely accepted, Squirrel was not average.

The speed and rapid changes were perfectly in tune to Squirrel's overactive mind and eyes. He stood, mouth gaping, as he stared at odd triangular object suspended above his head. Squirrel couldn't shake the feeling that he had seen this thing before. He had felt this thing before. It had watched him earlier today outside the fast food restaurant.

Squirrel turned to run back to Andy's house. His parents could spend the night worried about their son's dietary deviance for all he cared. Hell, he'd even eat a damn cheeseburger if Andy would let him back in the house. Squirrel made it two steps towards his friend's house before he was awash in an intense blue light. His mind screamed for him to move and run, but his body seemed incapable or unwilling to comply. After a few seconds in the light, these thoughts vanished. Squirrel felt relaxed, his mind oddly quiet. He let the feeling wash through his body, his muscles unknotting and going loose. Squirrel's mind silenced its constant chatter and white noise. This feeling was peaceful and tranquil. It was everything that Squirrel's unmedicated ADHD addled brain hated. He began to thrash and fight, as he was lifted higher and higher off of the ground.

Squirrel's flailing spun him over to his back where he saw a large circle open in the middle of the strange thing.

"No! No! No!" Squirrel yelled as he tried to swim away from the opening. It closed around him with a gentle mechanical *whoosh*. Squirrel began to scream, but no sounds escaped the object. A dirty Birkenstock sandal fell to the street with a dull *clunk* and Squirrel was gone.

-8-

Bovine subjects were so much easier to work with. They were docile and easily led even before they were exposed to the calming blue light. Human ones tended to be about the same, but this new subject was demonstrating some aberrant behaviors. The blue light actually appeared to be agitating the subject instead of calming it. The passenger had never observed this before and struggled to come up with an explanation. A desire to solve this quandary suddenly overwhelmed the passenger, muting its desire to study the spread of the blight.

"How is it that you are able to remain agitated while in the blue light?" the passenger asked in perfectly phrased English. Each word was precise and measured.

"What?" the subject screeched. "How? What the hell is going on?"

"I am sure that you find this situation," the passenger paused, "disconcerting, but please tell me how you are able to resist the influence of the light."

"Disconcerting?" the subject yelled. "That's putting it lightly!"

"Please remain still for a moment," the passenger commanded. A blinding neon green light appeared. Its beam was no bigger than the width of a pencil and it centered on the subject's forehead. "Your name is Abraham," the passenger continued, "but you prefer to be referred to as Squirrel. Strange that you would choose to be known by the title of a tree dwelling rodent, but yet when I see your thoughts that is what you prefer. Is that correct?"

"Uh, yeah. Pretty much everyone calls me that," Squirrel answered, unsure of what was occurring or if it was even real.

The small creature standing at the end of the table looked to be no more than five feet tall. Its pale gray skin glistened under the harsh lights. Thousands of tiny iridescent scales covered the creature's body and oversized head. Squirrel had seen countless drawings on TV scrawled by backwoods folk claiming to have been abducted and molested by little gray aliens and was shocked to find out just how right they were. Two small red pockets swelled like tiny balloons on the side of the thing's neck. They pulsed as each breath escaped the creature's minuscule nostrils. Huge, lidless eyes that shone like polished obsidian studied Squirrel with curiosity. A tight lipless smile stretched across the little gray man's wide face that tapered to a narrow beak-like point.

Oddly, Squirrel did not feel threatened by the creature, but still felt the urge to scream. A question, at first small and bothersome like a cut on the roof of Squirrel's mouth worried him. The question quickly grew, filling Squirrel's head until it was all he could focus on.

"Are you going to probe me?" Squirrel demanded. "I mean, anally?"

The passenger sighed and pressed a few buttons on a nearby control panel. The table shifted, slowly falling away like a pile of tiny marbles. Squirrel found himself now sitting in a chair.

"Why does your kind have such a preoccupation with probing that region?" the passenger asked. "There is nothing to be learned from studying that area. At least not anything that would benefit the current situation."

"So you're not going to probe me?" Squirrel asked tentatively.

"I guess, I could program my ship's system to accommodate that request," the passenger answered. It turned and began pressing a few more buttons on the panel.

"OWW! OWW!" Squirrel shrieked as he leapt up from the seat. "I didn't want you to do that. Jeez, man, I was just making sure you weren't going to."

"My apologies. You seemed disappointed," the passenger nodded. "Please go back to your seat. I have disabled the program."

"Much appreciated, uh, um…guy," Squirrel said as he slowly lowered himself into the chair.

"Guy?" the passenger smirked. "No, that is not my name, but you are welcome to refer to me by that title, nonetheless."

"Well, then what is your name?" Squirrel asked.

A high-pitched sounded cut through Squirrel's brain. Tears involuntarily spilled from his eyes as he gnashed his teeth.

"That," the passenger nodded. "I realize that it must have sounded unpleasant. My people's language is difficult for your kind to hear, but you did ask."

"That's your language?" Squirrel cried, echoes of the awful sound still rattling his brain. "But you were speaking English. Don't you have a name that I can understand?"

"Yes," the passenger responded. "I can speak English, but no, I don't have a name in that dialect."

"But then, why do you use it then?" Squirrel asked.

"Because that is the one that your kind tends to demand others use," the passenger answered. "Even in areas where your language is not native, you still seem determined to require others to use it."

"Yeah, I guess that's true," Squirrel admitted. "But it's not like I can just screech at you when I want your attention. So what can I call you?"

The passenger thought for a moment. "You had called me 'guy' before. That is a name amongst your people, is it not?"

"Sure, a bad one," Squirrel laughed, "but hey, what the hell. Guy, it is."

"Very good then," Guy smiled thinly. "So now that the formalities are out of the way, let us get to the real reason I have required your company."

"Damn it!" Squirrel yelled. He pointed an angry finger at Guy. "I knew you were going to anally probe me! Had to get me to relax, huh? You lying alien molester! Leave my b-hole alone!" Squirrel angrily shook his fist and clenched his butt cheeks.

"No one is going to probe your anus!" Guy shouted. He stomped his foot with a wet slap. "I have no interest in your...*your* b-hole*! What I require is your blood."

"My blood?" Squirrel said, regretting his words. "Maybe we could reconsider the whole probing of the anal region thing. I mean blood seems a bit extreme."

"I only require a small amount," Guy explained. "No more than a pin prick. A drop really."

"A drop?" Squirrel reiterated. "I guess, I can do that, but why? What are you going to learn from one drop of my blood?"

"I need to know how much of the blight you have in your system," Guy continued. "I need to know how bad the situation is."

"What the hell is the *blight* and how did it get in my system?" Squirrel snapped.

"Your kind has been manufacturing it through a misunderstood series of steps stolen from my peoples' technology," Guy answered. "It is a leftover from the harvesting of bovine flesh. I believe it is known as LFTB among your kind."

"LFTB?" Squirrel asked. "That sounds like some sort of lesbians' rights coalition. Are aliens a bunch of homophobes or something? I'm not having anything to do with some fascist, right wing extraterrestrial agenda."

"Lesbians?" Guy repeated, turning his head slightly sideways. "No, this has nothing to do with lesbians. It would probably surprise you to know that humans are among the only creatures left that actually care about sexual orientation. The rest of the universe does not care about such trivial things."

"Okay, good," Squirrel nodded, "because I'm not joining some intergalactic branch of Scientology or anything."

Guy laughed. "Trust me, only creatures on your planet are interested in converting people to that faith. Honestly, the rest of us find it humorous and misinformed. No, LFTB is something worse than even Scientology. I believe most humans refer to it by its more commonly known slang name – pink slime."

"Pink slime?" Squirrel snorted. "You won't find any of that in my blood or system or whatever. I'm a vegetarian, man. I have been my whole life. I don't eat beef."

"Crap," Guy sighed. "I detected high concentrations of the pink slime in the dwelling you exited. I thought that it was you."

"No, it wasn't me. Couldn't have been," Squirrel replied. He knew that Guy must have detected Andy, but was not going to tell him about his friend until he was sure that the alien meant Andy no harm. "But why do you care about humans eating some low grade beef ooze?"

"Because it is not beef," Guy said, his large black eyes flashed with intensity. "It is something far more dangerous than a cheeseburger."

A thick string of chocolate-laced drool had run down Andy's chin and hardened. He groaned and rubbed the back of his hand across his cheeks and chins. Flecks of sugary chocolate saliva flaked off and gently fluttered down onto his belly.

Andy had fallen asleep in the basement, as usual. He had a room, a bed and all the normal things a person should own, but for some reason, he always found himself waking up in the loveseat in the basement. It was probably because he spent most nights down there living in the electronic alternate universe offered by his Xbox, but some piece of him knew it was also because he had outgrown his twin bed. The last time Andy had slept upstairs, the bed creaked with uncertainty and strain. He could have moved the large queen sized bed from his mother's old bedroom into his, but he didn't like going into that room. She had hung herself in the closet there. Memories of finding her hanging, blue lipped, bug eyed and dangling among her dresses with a pair of Andy's underwear wrapped around her neck still haunted him. He was in no rush to revisit these unhappy times from his childhood.

Besides, the loveseat had become form fitted, perfectly cradling both Andy and his bulk. The center springs had collapsed inward after hours of endless gaming, creating a polyester nest for Andy. This was this throne and the basement his kingdom. It was the only place where Andy was allowed to be more than his appearance. Where he could be the hero and rescue the princess. But without fail these computer generated escapes would end, morning would come and Andy would have to return to work and normal life where he was little more than a living joke.

Andy fished a semi-clean work shirt out of the hamper and snapped it over his head. He noticed that the flab under his arm had grown significantly since the last time he checked. Flicking the loose bag of flesh, Andy counted fourteen seconds before it stopped rhythmically undulating.

"Great," Andy sneered, "now I can time things with my arm fat." He wondered what one of his ass cheeks would clock in around. Probably the duration of a movie and not just one of those ninety-minute Hollywood cookie cutter crap fests. No, Andy was fairly certain that following a gentle flick, his ass cheek could probably dance through an epic. Images of those blue wave things people kept on their desks flooded Andy's mind as he fought the urge to spank his own butt.

As he pulled the shirt over his head, Andy felt something hard and crusty slide over his cheek and neck.

"What the hell?" Andy groaned as he looked in the cracked mirror that hung above the washing machine. He was yet to understand why his mother had hung it there or why Rachel left it. Maybe it served as a constant reminder of what their lives had amounted to, almost a daily affirmation of just how low a suburban existence can drag someone who was unexceptional. This was probably what drove his mother to hang herself. Andy hoped that it wouldn't do the same to Rachel, but still found himself unable to take the mirror down.

"Freaking cheese?" Andy asked his reflection as he picked at the hardened yellow stain on the collar of his shirt. He must have worn this shirt last week. It had been National Hot Dog Day. All chili cheese dogs were buy three, get one free. Andy lost count after his fourth free hotdog. He picked at the hardened cheese sauce, but it refused to budge. There was no way that Andy was walking into the Jock Itch with that on his shirt. Todd would hone onto the stain like a shark smelling blood in the water. Andy would never hear the end of it. But he was out of shirts.

Andy sighed loudly, pulled his collar forward and jammed it into his mouth. He was flooded with self-loathing as he sucked the old hardened cheese from his shirt. Was this really what his life had come to? Should he really be surprised that it had? As the salty goodness of the synthetic cheese filled his mouth, Andy's feelings numbed and he forget to hate himself for a few minutes.

"Andy, come get breakfast!" Rachel shouted from the top of the basement stairs. "It's getting cold!"

"Mum com in'" Andy mumbled. He had forgotten that his shirt was still in his mouth.

"Huh?" Rachel barked. "I don't have time for your crazy alien video game languages. Beep bo bop bo, Andy! That means get your butt up here and eat your frigging breakfast."

"Okay, okay!" Andy called back. He reached up and pulled string to turn off the bulb that hung above the washing machine. His arm fat swung in time with the light bulb and chain. The rhythm of his arm flab momentarily hypnotized Andy. It jiggled all the time. He couldn't remember a time when it didn't, but it seemed to really be feeling the music today. Was it that big yesterday, Andy wondered? He didn't think so, but could he really have gotten fatter in one night? Andy figured, if anyone could that he could. Every child dreamed of having super powers. Evidently Andy's was the amazing ability to become wigglier with each day.

"Have no fear, the Human Jam Jar is here," Andy wheezed as he began to climb the stairs. "Sleep well, citizens, I've come to stop evil in its tracks with my amazing ability to...to...jiggle." Tears stung Andy's eyes. Joking worked most of the time. Defusing other people's jokes by stealing the punch lines was a great preemptive strategy, but did little when the person making fun of Andy was himself. The stairs creaked under Andy's feet.

"Andy!" Rachel bellowed from the kitchen.

"I'm on my way, damn it!" Andy stamped his foot. The stair cracked and buckled inward with a deafening snap. The splintered wood grabbed at Andy's ankle and pulled it inward. "Crap!" Andy yelled, but stopped himself from calling for his sister. She would use this as a lesson, as a chance to chide Andy about his weight and eating habits.

"What was that?" Rachel asked.

"Nothing!" Andy shouted, "I'll be there in a second!" He grabbed his leg and pulled. Splinters bit into his soft flesh, but he continued to pull. A little pain now was a hell of a lot better than the pain brought on by one of Rachel's lectures.

Andy's leg popped free. Shards of wood speckled his pants. The lower part of his pants leg was wet, but it didn't look like blood. After brushing the stair fragments off his jeans, Andy examined his fingers. They felt slimy and sticky, but there was no sign of blood.

"Whatever," Andy groaned as he finished climbing the stairs. He evidently wasn't hurt, at least not physically.

"Oatmeal," Rachel smiled as she placed the bowl in front of Andy. "Make sure you eat it, okay? I have to get to work and I don't want to find it in the garbage."

"Yeah, yeah, yeah," Andy waved with his spoon. He had no intention of eating the oatmeal. It tasted like paste.

"Please, Andy," Rachel pleaded as she shouldered her bag and headed for the door. "Please, no fast food today?"

"Okay," Andy smiled. "I won't go in the food fast place today." He knew he was twisting her words, but also didn't want to lie to his sister. Going through the drive thru didn't require going inside, so technically speaking, Andy told the truth.

"Good," Rachel smiled sadly. She knew he was lying.

As soon as Andy heard Rachel's car start, he dumped the oatmeal in the garbage, buried it beneath some scraps of paper and vegetable peels and headed for his car.

If your day started with your oversized ankle and foot falling through one of the basement steps, well, then damn it, a breakfast sandwich or three was definitely warranted, no matter how much oatmeal your sister made.

-10-

Squirrel lost track of how long he had been in Guy's ship. With no windows or clocks, time lost its relevance. All Squirrel could focus on was the little gray man scuttling back and forth in front him.

"We need to figure out how the blight has concentrated so highly in this area," Guy said to himself as he punched keys. Screens emerged from the wall, seemingly materializing from nowhere. The little alien stared at them intently, studying the patterns. Small red dots were scattered across the screen. Some were larger than others.

The largest was directly over Andy's house, but Squirrel still had yet to tell Guy about his friend's dangerous dietary persuasions. Squirrel felt relatively sure that he was safe or at least that his rectum was, but he still wasn't going to sell out his one and only friend to some intergalactic health inspector.

"So what," Squirrel began, as he stood up from the metallic chair. It was cool like metal, but completely fluid and malleable to his body. "This blight it's like some kind of fungus or something?"

"Not exactly," Guy answered turning to face Squirrel. Even though the alien's smooth, lipless face and cold eyes betrayed little emotion, Squirrel could see whatever Guy was thinking was causing him some hesitation. "It's more of a parasite. Some time ago, my people were trying to rid themselves of the blight, but lacked the proper means and environment to do so. The blight was an organism we bioengineered to break down the high amounts of waste on our planet. It was designed to digest all refuse and then become dormant after a certain amount of organic waste passed through its simple system. It obviously did not work. The blight began infecting my people and decomposing them. It passed from one to another through touch and almost wiped out my entire race."

"Whoa! Whoa! Wait a minute," Squirrel cut in. "Are you telling me that you dropped some alien STD that your scientists created on Earth? See, that right there, man. You can't go around playing God. Mother Nature only likes to have one cook in the kitchen, bro."

"We had no other choice," Guy admitted. "But no, it wasn't me who brought the blight to Earth to be disposed of. I believe it was approximately the Earth year 1947 when we attempted to dispose of the blight. We had since explored other nations and regions, but none proved as naturally diverse as the United States of America, so logically, it was the most ideal place to test disposal methods. The most promising plan was to expose it to the extreme temperatures and lack of water within one of your desert regions. Knowing the design of the blight, we assumed that exposure to varied extreme temperatures and a lack of food would destroy the organism."

"So you decided to dump your toxic waste in our country?" Squirrel growled. "What gives you the right? Because you're so much more advanced than us, huh?"

"Is that so different from the practices your government engages in now in third world countries?" Guy asked. His words were honest, not accusatory. Squirrel had to admit that the alien had a point.

"Before, you said 1947?" Squirrel asked. "Were you talking about...?"

"Roswell, New Mexico," Guy nodded, finishing the thought. "We were less than successful. Some of the blight escaped while in transit and the ship carrying it crashed near a cattle farm. The blight was introduced into the cows nearby and the results were...unpredictable to say the least."

"How does it survive inside a cow?" Squirrel demanded. "Shouldn't it just rot the cow and then turn off?"

"In theory, yes," Guy agreed, "but we had not anticipated the interior environment of the bovine stomach or should I say stomachs. Few other creatures in the universe have more than one stomach, let alone four. This unique adaption allowed the bovine population to pass the blight safely from one stomach to the next until it became part of them. The side effect of this is that the cows produced more milk, grew faster and could ultimately be broken down into what you call pink slime. To the uniformed, these aforementioned side effects seem desirable, but your government did not heed our warnings about allowing the blight to spread too widely. We had in fact, pushed for them to sterilize the infected bovine population. They thin the numbers of infected cows from time to time under the guise of Mad Cow, but it is nowhere near what is required to control the blight."

"So our government knows that Americans have been eating this crap since the 1950s and isn't doing anything to stop it," Squirrel snapped. "Typical! Just freaking typical!"

"The crew of the downed ship was taken into custody by your government," Guy continued. "They warned them about the blight, but your government did not listen."

"They're like that," Squirrel agreed. "But did they know it would get this bad?"

"No," Guy shook his bulbous head. A miniature light show occurred in each tiny scale that blanketed Guy's head. "Your scientists, along with ours, determined that the side effects were a benefit to your people, so long as the blight was controlled. In later years though, your government ceased to listen and allowed farmers to introduce steroids and growth hormones into the bovine population. This also strengthened the blight, but your government wrongly assumed that no American could consume enough beef flesh to actually feel the effects of it. Clearly, your alarming obesity rates and unsafe food practices indicate otherwise."

"So what?" Squirrel replied. "Now you're here to try to fix your mistake? To try to clean up the mess your little science experiment created?"

"I would again ask you, Squirrel, if that is so different from what your own people do?" Guy questioned. "Is that really so different from how your people acted after your second world conflict? Once the devastation of your experiment was visited upon Japan, did you not rush over to try to bury your shame beneath the foundations of new buildings?"

"Damn," Squirrel nodded. "Is debate and Earth history a core class for aliens or something?"

Guy let out something that sounded like a high-pitched squeak. From the movement of the alien's slender shoulders, Squirrel assumed it was a laugh. But before Guy could fully respond, an alarm began beeping erratically on one of the ship's many screens.

"The highest concentration of the blight is moving away from the neighborhood," Guy reported. "It looks like it is headed towards your commerce area."

"You mean downtown," Squirrel nodded. "Yeah, I know exactly where it is going." As the largest red dot on the screen crossed the street to what Squirrel knew was The Jock Itch, he couldn't pretend anymore.

"Guy?" Squirrel asked. "What would happen to a person who had that much pink slime in them?"

"I am not sure," Guy said honestly. "This is more than we have ever seen within one subject. It is…it is…" The alien paused to think. How could this much of the blight have amassed in the system of a single organism?

"It's Andy," Squirrel said, his words heavy and sad.

-11-

The morning shift at the Jock Itch was awful. There really was no other adjective to describe a morning spent with Todd. Andy detested the duties of the morning shift, but following his string of sick days and the dressing room incident, Jim had demanded that Andy take the hours no one else wanted. Todd, not wanting to miss a chance to torture Andy, gladly switched his shift.

"What up Tig Bitties?" Todd smirked. "I know I told you I like my D's doubled, but I meant on chicks."

"And here I thought it was because that was the highest you could get in the alphabet," Andy mumbled. He knew antagonizing Todd was a bad idea, a terrible one in fact, but he found himself feeling oddly aggressive. The emotion was completely out of character for Andy. Maybe it was because his morning had started so crappy. Maybe he was just tired of Todd's shit. Everyone had a breaking point. Maybe this was Andy's.

"What'd you say, jelly jugs?" Todd reached out to flick Andy's chest, something he did almost on a daily basis. Andy was used to this. What he was not used to was the way his chest undulated, rippling like waves of bread dough. "Wow, you're really getting fat there, Candy Andy. That's almost a talent."

"Shut up, Todd," Andy muttered, but all of the anger had drained from his voice. It was nearly impossible to be threatening when your man boobs were busy hula dancing.

"Yeah, whatever, doughboy," Todd snapped. "Waddle your big ass into the stock room and inventory the new shipment of Under Armor. Try not to leave your floury fingerprints all over the ladies underwear while you're sniffing it. I mean folding it. Okay?"

Andy wanted to tell Todd to shove it. To tell him to go look for his steroid-shrunken testicles. Andy wanted to tell him that and more, but what came out was, "Um, okay, Todd." With that statement of defeat, Andy slowly made his way to the stock room. At least, if he were back there counting dry-wick sports bras, he wouldn't have to suffer any of Todd's abuse.

A dry cough rattled deep in Andy's chest. It rumbled and then exploded from his mouth with the ferocity of a car backfiring. A wad of pinkish phlegm arced through the air and crashed onto the floor with a wet *splat*.

"Great," Andy coughed. Another clump of the disgusting snot dangled from his lower lip. "Now I can add a head cold to an already craptastic day."

Andy's stomach seized, tying itself in burning knots. Fiery iron clamps clinched Andy's guts and twisted with the force of an over-caffeinated T-Rex. Andy's hands instinctively cradled his stomach. Something thick and disgusting burbled up from Andy's stomach and burned the back of his throat. His head throbbed, threatening to split open.

"Oh God," Andy groaned as sat down and held his head. He wanted to rest it on his knees, to curl into a little ball. But his knees were buried beneath his considerable gut, so Andy rested his head there. His stomach felt soft, felt comfortable.

"I tell you to do inventory and find you back here trying to blow yourself?" Todd shouted. "Give it up tons of fun. You wouldn't even be able to find your teeny weenie underneath all that Jell-O."

"Fuck you, Todd," Andy snarled. The words made his head hurt even worse, but he felt unable to keep them inside. Rage boiled inside him.

"Suddenly found a pair, huh?" Todd stepped forward. His shoulders squared as he puffed his chest out and tried to appear more imposing. "Grew a few hairs last night and suddenly someone's a man."

"Piss off, asshole," Andy snapped. "I don't have the patience for your stupidity today. Go work on figuring out how to tie your shoes. That should keep you busy for the rest of the day, you stupid, over-juiced moron!"

"Stupid?" Todd sneered. His fists balled into tight fists. "Did you just call me stupid?" His words were raw. Andy had found Todd's sensitive spot.

"Sorry," Andy said as he climbed to his feet. His guts and head still throbbed with pangs of hot pain. "Did I say it too fast? Should I have tried to find another way to say that you are the biggest idiot this side of a room full of gas huffing monkeys?"

Todd's fist landed squarely in Andy's stomach. Pain exploded and radiated through Andy's body, but was quickly buried beneath his anger, his anger and an undeniable urge to vomit. Andy stopped fighting and released his stomach's contents.

Hot, thick strings of pink goo covered Todd's face and shoulders. Andy was shocked by the ferocity with which he puked. He had seen projectile vomit in horror movies, but never thought that he was possible of the same.

Todd gagged, his fingers splayed out in disgust. The vomit hung in thick, ropey strings from his ears and chin, dancing with each disgusted shudder that passed through his body. A heavy ball of the viscous puke slipped from his shoulder and splattered onto the hard concrete floor of the stock room.

"What is this?" Todd screeched. "What did you eat? Are you full of strawberry milkshake? You are so gross, so frigging gross! God, you...you..."

Andy prepared for Todd's attack, but it never came. Todd's words trailed off, his mouth hung open in shock, as he turned to walk out of the store room, leaving a gelled pink trail in his wake. The bells on the front door chimed as Todd left the Jock Itch.

"Go figure?" Andy smirked. He actually felt better. Todd would surely be gone for the rest shift. Maybe the day was actually starting to turn around?

-12-

The object slowly turned as it dropped lower and lower to the ground. The grass underneath bent and lay flat, forming a wide circle.

"I do apologize," Guy shrugged.

"For what?" Squirrel asked as he pushed himself up from the strange morphing chair.

"The discomfort you will experience in what you call your 'b-hole' during the violent probing of your anal region. I am sorry but it must commence before I release you," Guy stated flatly. He reached into an opening in the wall that had only moments before not been there and withdrew a fourteen-inch long white pole with small blinking studs peppering the sides. Guy flicked a button and the head of the probe began whipping about violently. "This will go better if you hold still and try to relax."

"You rotten bastard!" Squirrel shrieked as he backed away from Guy. "I knew it! I knew this was all about my b-hole!"

A thin lipless smile suddenly appeared on Guy's smooth face. His shoulders hitched a little as a laugh burst from his mouth.

"Sorry," Guy smirked, "I could not resist an attempt at what you humans call humor. Did it work?"

"Humor?"

"Yes, Squirrel," Guy nodded. "As I have stated before, I have no interest in probing your *b-hole*. I promise you there is nothing up there that I want to study."

"Then what is that giant space dildo for?" Squirrel asked, still unsure of what Guy's intentions were. "Are aliens like really into sex toys or something?"

"Sex toys?" Guy repeated, not knowing what Squirrel was referring to. "This is not for probing or sexual activity, though I do think a desire to engage in alien sex is why humans have created this myth about anal probing. No, this is nothing more a device for removing clogs from my waste disposal system."

"Like a plunger?" Squirrel questioned.

"Nothing more," Guy nodded. "But I do apologize for having to drop you off so far from your dwelling. It would be imprudent not to do so and risk being seen. I do hope you understand." Guy

38

pressed a series of small red buttons. The wall behind Squirrel melted away to form a long sloping ramp. "I will be in contact with you soon, but for now, you must go to your friend and attempt to dissuade him from consuming any further amounts of the pink slime."

"What's going to happen to Andy?" Squirrel asked over his shoulder from where he stood on the ramp. "Is he going to be okay?"

"I am honestly not sure," Guy said. "He has ingested a great deal of the blight and there is no telling what it is doing to his system. It could alter his behavior and quite possibly his physiology. We must act quickly."

"Alter him?" Squirrel repeated. "Like mutate or something?"

"Yes," Guy answered. "I am sorry, Squirrel. I know that he is your friend."

"My only one," Squirrel said sadly.

"Not anymore," Guy added. "You are not alone in this, Squirrel. My people are as responsible for this as is your government. I will do whatever is within my power to help you and save your friend."

"Thank you," Squirrel grinned. "I had better get going though, because if I know Andy, then he is on his way to stuff his face with more pink slime."

Squirrel started down the newly appeared ramp, but stopped to admire the massive crop circle that had been created around the object.

"You guys actually go around making crop circles?" Squirrel asked. "I thought that was just people screwing around. Are they for communication or something?"

"Communication?" Guy snorted. "No, it's just something we do to mess with humans."

"More alien humor?" Squirrel added. "Like the whole probe thing?"

"You are correct, Squirrel," Guy nodded. "You should examine some of the aerial photos of our crop circles."

"Why?" Squirrel asked, looking at the circle. It was a large circle with smaller lines edging inwards, almost giving it the appearance of the puckered end of a hotdog. "What the hell are they going to look like beyond a giant circle?" But as the words left his mouth, Squirrel already knew the answer.

"B-holes," the boy and alien said in unison.

"Lovely," Squirrel muttered as he walked down the ramp. "You made a massive balloon knot, huh? That's just wonderful."

With that thought in mind, Squirrel walked down the ramp to stand in the middle of a giant brown eye. He couldn't shake the feeling that where he currently found himself was a sign, a rectal omen of how everything was going to work out.

"How appropriate," Squirrel moped. "My best friend is full of some crazy pink space goo and the only person I've got to help me is an extraterrestrial who thinks it's hilarious to fly millions of light years to draw a giant butt hole in the middle of a corn field. I'm screwed...totally and completely screwed."

-13-

The rest of Andy's day at the Jock Itch passed without incident. Working Todd-free turned out to be pretty enjoyable. Andy spent the day reorganizing the swimsuit issues on the magazine rack and watching old episodes of Star Trek on YouTube.

A few customers came in the store to buy random athletic gear that they would most likely never use. This was the cornerstone of Jim's economic plan for the Jock Itch. After working for a few weeks, Andy had come to realize that what people bought at stores like the Jock Itch wasn't sneakers or sweatpants. It was hope and optimism. Granted both the shoes and resolutions were cheaply made and would soon be broken or forgotten, but Andy could empathize with these people. They were addicted to glamour magazines and suffered all of the airbrush related lowering of self-esteem that came along with every fake glossy photo. Andy understood what it was like to be completely reliant upon the very thing that was destroying you.

A sudden urge to set the magazine rack on fire flooded Andy's mind. *Just burn it! Burn the whole store!* The thought seemed to come from nowhere, operating under its own volition. Andy could end it, could release these people and save them from themselves with the cleansing touch of fire.

"No! No! No! That'd be wrong!" Andy shouted to himself.

A middle aged woman three aisles away cast an offended look in Andy's direction before putting down a pair of neon green stretch pants and picking up a pair of larger plain black sweats.

Andy shook the ideas of arson from his head. Burning down the Jock Itch and all the magazines inside wouldn't set these people free. They would just go online or find another store, because the truth was that these people didn't want to be saved. On some sick level, people enjoyed torturing themselves, twisting themselves into the fractured molds that Hollywood and Us Weekly forced upon them.

A moment of panic squeezed Andy's heart as thoughts of his favorite restaurant being reduced to a smoldering pile of ashes danced through his brain. Would that stop Andy from slowly killing himself with each mouthful of what some part of him knew was poison, but couldn't bring himself to put down? No, Andy would find another restaurant in another town or simply go to the supermarket and fill his freezer with the same crap. Andy would never stop. He had surrendered long ago and so had all the customers milling about in the Jock Itch.

A loud burbling groan rumbled from deep within Andy's considerable belly. Working without Todd was wonderful, but it also meant that Andy didn't get a lunch break. Chewing on chalky protein bars did little to silence the monkey on Andy's back that demanded the salty sweet goodness found wrapped in greasy paper and at the bottom of oversized waxed paper cups.

"Damn," Andy growled as he cupped his gut. He had been hungry before. Hell, he existed in a permanent state of hunger, but this was unlike anything he had ever experienced. He was starving.

Tearing open a box of energy bars, Andy grabbed a fistful of the little granola bricks and shredded the wrappers. He shoved four of the bars into his mouth, chewing angrily, bits of food caking the corner of his mouth.

"Tastes like dog turds," Andy grumped. His stomach growled its agreement. This was not what Andy wanted. This did not satiate his hunger. A massive bubble popped in Andy's stomach.

"Oh, man," Andy wheezed as he doubled over. The urge to vomit gripped his guts once again. Could he be so hungry that he felt nauseous? Or maybe it was those gross little power bars? Who really knew what all the organic, cane juice, pure squeezed whatever really did to your body?

"*Purrrup!*" Andy belched. A phlegmy bubble popped in the back of his throat. Small pink dots speckled the glass counter near the cash register. "What the hell?" Andy murmured as he connected the greasy dots with his fingers. They left large slimy pink trails.

"Um, excuse me," the middle aged woman said impatiently. "Am I going to be able to check out some time today?"

Andy looked up, recognizing the woman. It was Kristen Spiel. She was a middle-aged, two-time divorcee that frequented the Jock Itch, always seeking some new clothing or workout program to help recapture her lost youth. She was attractive, but hid it underneath layer upon layer of cheap drugstore makeup. Andy always thought what Kristen needed wasn't a new work out or pair of stretch pants. What she needed was some makeup remover and a washcloth. Everyone who worked at the Jock Itch, Andy included, suspected Kristen was after more than clothes being that she always seemed to show up when Todd was working.

"Yeah, sorry, Ms. Spiel," Andy nodded and took her clothes.

"It's Kristen," she answered. "You should know better than to make a lady feel old."

"Right," Andy responded. "Kristen. Sorry. Anything else I can help you with today?" Andy passed her a black and white striped plastic bag that held Kristen's purchase.

"Um," Kristen hesitated. Andy knew what she was going to ask, but wasn't going to make her cradle robbing any easier. "So, um, well. No. I mean, not unless you know when Todd is coming back."

"Todd wasn't feeling well today," Andy snapped. He could feel anger roiling up inside him. A loud gurgle rumbled through his gut. Andy's stomach vibrated slightly. He caught Kristen's eyes darting to his belly. His anger flared with a newfound rage.

"Oh, no," Kristen feigned. "I hope he's okay. He didn't come down with anything serious, did he?"

"Not sure," Andy sneered. "How serious are your sexually transmissible diseases?"

"You fat nasty bast-" Kristen began to scream, but her words were cut short by the steaming torrent of pink vomit that erupted from Andy's mouth. The upchuck caked Kristen's hair in tangled, foul smelling dreadlocks and spilled down her throat. She opened her mouth to scream, but the words were silenced by her disgust. The bells on the door chimed joyfully as Kristen tore out of the Jock Itch.

"Thanks for shopping at The Jock Itch. Come again," Andy grinned as he wiped a few errant strings of vomit that swung lazily from his chin. "Probably time to close up shop anyway." Andy turned off the lights and locked the store's doors, completely unaware of the small globules of pink goo peppered the floor and inched along behind him.

Andy's mind raced with what had happen today, but oddly enough, he didn't find it upsetting or disconcerting. He felt justified. Angry and justified. And hungry. Andy felt very, very hungry.

-14-

Todd was pissed. He was super pissed, like the kind of pissed he felt at the gym when some weak asshole wouldn't get off *his* bench. No, this was even worse. This was a whole new kind of pissed, reserved only for the most extreme situations of disrespect.

Todd was an alpha male. He knew it. He went out of his way to make sure everyone else knew, especially Candy Andy. That loser wasn't even a beta male on his best day. Andy was the absolute opposite of everything Todd knew a man should be. Todd was a Man, capital 'M'. Andy was…was…well, he was just Andy. Did Todd even really have to explain how he was so much better than him? But then why was a small voice nagging in the back of his mind? Why did some small piece of Todd feel intimidated by Andy? He had never felt that way before and now was gripped by a growing sense that Andy could do terrible things to him.

That pile of lard had puked all over him. Sure, that had been bad enough, but it was just gross, that was all. Right? *Shouldn't that have just made me angry,* Todd wondered.

Todd tossed back and forth on his bed, the sheets drenched with sweat and tangled around his legs. Whatever that load that Andy had been sick with was wreaking havoc in Todd's body. He felt feverish and sweaty one minute, and then nauseous and cold the next.

"Tig Bitties gave me the flu," Todd groaned as he rolled over and coughed into his hand. It was a wet hacking cough. "When I get back to work, I'm gonna punish that pile of fat." A second cough. Something wet and sticky lumped in Todd's hand.

Todd opened his hand to see a large wad of pink phlegm in his palm. It looked like the crap that Candy Andy had puked all over him earlier today. The thought that maybe he had swallowed some of Andy's puke shuddered through Todd. No, it couldn't be that. He must just have whatever Andy had, that was all.

Being sick was not something Todd was accustomed to. Sickness was weakness, plain and simple, and Todd wasn't weak. He could beat this. He was better than this cold or flu or whatever. And he sure as hell was better than Andy.

The simple act of dropping his legs over the side of the bed sent hot waves of pain dancing through Todd's over muscled body. He forced himself to stand. It was time for a reality check. It was time to take control. Time to man up.

There was large full-length mirror on the inside of Todd's closet door. Usually, he kept it open so he could easily catch a glimpse of himself when he came home from gym, but the door was closed. His mom must have been in here cleaning again.

"Stupid cow," Todd growled, echoing his father, as he stormed towards the closet door. Todd grabbed the handle and threw open the closet door. Something was wrong. Something looked off. It must be a trick of the lights or his fever or both.

Todd flicked the nearby light switch, turning on the overhead light. His breath caught in his throat.

Todd's nose had dropped out of place, appeared to be slowly running down his face. His ears and cheeks were doing the same. It was like watching plastic melt in slow motion.

With trembling hands, Todd tried to push his nose back into place. It moved back with little resistance.

"There," Todd said, his voice devoid of conviction. His eyes widened as he watched his nose once again resume its journey towards his chin. Come to think of it, now it looked like his chin was slowly slipping downward as well.

"I'm melting?" Todd's voice trembled. He held his hands up before his face. The skin appeared almost translucent, a slight pink tinge to it that spoke nothing of health. The lamp on the dresser behind Todd illuminated the back of his hand. The shadowy silhouette of the finger bones wiggled in the mirror.

"Mom?" Todd said weakly, suddenly feeling like a child again. The skin on his fingers sloughed and slipped, running together, giving his Todd's hands a webbed appearance. "Mom?" Todd's voice cracked once more before countless pink bubbles frothed in his throat, choking his words.

Todd's knees felt weak. He couldn't tell if it was from his skin liquefying or his nerves, but either way, Todd found himself collapsing slowly to the floor.

Minutes bled into hours. Todd had no idea how long he lay on the floor unconscious. Slowly, Todd's vision came back into focus, but he felt like he was staring through a strawberry Jell-O mold. Why was everything tinted pink?

"Mom?" Todd groaned as he stood up, but words sounded muffled. A thick viscous bubble popped near Todd's shoulder and spattered the mirror with flecks of goo that resembled spoiled strawberry jam. Todd stared at the greasy spots on his mirror. His hand shot up to whip away the slime, but he only smeared more of the ooze across the surface.

Suddenly, the image in the mirror dawned on Todd. What was this thing staring back at him? How could this thing be standing in his place? A skeleton suspended in pink slime glared back at Todd from within the mirror. A wicked rictus grin stretched across the skeleton's face from within the pile of burbling ooze. Slowly, the realization that this disgusting monster *was* Todd crept into his mind. He wanted to feel scared or panicked or anything that made sense, but Todd felt none of these emotions.

Somewhere from deep inside of Todd's mind, something called out to him, beckoned for him to join it. He belonged. Now all he had to do was find whatever called to him.

Todd pulled his foot up from the floor. The thick carpet tugged and pulled at the bottoms of Todd's feet as he slowly made his way towards the door. He wanted, no needed, to find what called to him and nothing would stand in his way. The door opened, ropey pink strands dangling from the doorknob.

"Todd, is that you, honey? It sounds like you're feeling better," his mother called from the kitchen. "Are you hungry, sweetie? Why don't you come and eat? I made your favorite, fried chicken."

His mother's words sounded muffled, but the questions struck a note deep within Todd, deep within his guts, which now floated somewhere to the left of his ribcage.

Yes, Todd thought. He was hungry, hungrier than he had ever been in his life, but Todd had no interest in eating fried chicken. This kind of hunger could only be quelled by one thing.

-15-

Andy slammed his car door and headed towards the restaurant. His eyes darted around the parking lot. For some reason, Andy found himself feeling tense, uneasy, like the uncomfortable sensation experienced when someone stared at you from across a room. Andy knew he was being watched, but had no idea by whom. Maybe it was just all that crap Squirrel had said last time they were here? Maybe it was just Squirrel? He had the annoying knack for showing up and shattering the momentary beefy bliss Andy found between two delicious sesame seed buns. Andy was starving and the last thing he wanted screwing up his feast was Squirrel's hippy diatribe.

"Whatever," Andy shook his head, sure that no one in the parking lot was paying attention to him. Something in Andy screamed at him for being stupid, so quick to let his guard down. He needed to look everywhere, even up.

Brilliant oranges, yellows and pinks streaked across the sky, reminding Andy that he really wanted a strawberry shake. Thin wispy clouds were stretched across the vibrant backdrop like cotton balls on a child's art project. Andy studied the clouds. The corner of one appeared folded, bent at an unnatural angle. The wrinkle in the edge of the cloud rippled, as if trying to flatten itself.

Andy squinted. "What the hell? I must be really freaking hungry." Just a trick of the eye, Andy assured himself. He was hungry, really, really hungry and his eyes were just feeling the effects of his empty stomach. This was a problem that twenty dollars and the 99 cent menu could fix.

Pushing through the fingerprint smudged double doors, Andy found himself looking for Cece behind the counter, which was strange. Habit would normally cause Andy's eyes to immediately fixate on the menu hung above the counter, not the person behind. In truth, there was no reason for Andy to look at the menu. He had the entire thing, price included, committed to memory. Any exciting new additions like the recent return of the Rib-A-Q Sandwich, Andy knew about long before they were even slid into place on menu board from his online searches and chat rooms.

But today, for some reason, Andy found himself searching the restaurant for Cece. His hunger pangs lessened slightly as he thought he glimpsed her working behind the Fry-A-Lator, but came roaring back when he realized it was just some other employee with blonde hair and Cece's build.

"What am I doing?" Andy muttered to himself. Why was he suddenly more concerned with finding Cece, than he was with procuring his salty delights? Andy paused at the condiments station and tore open four ketchup packets. He squeezed them into his mouth as he thought about Cece, thought about the day he had walked in on her at the Jock Itch. Something screamed inside Andy's head. *FOOD! EAT! NOW!* The voice was a chorus of tiny angry screams, all yelling in unison.

Thoughts of Cece vanished as Andy stumbled towards the counter. His palms were sweating, beads forming and streaking down his hands. Andy crammed his hand into his pocket and fished for money. He had intended to get only twenty dollars worth of 99-cent value items, but his hand emerged with three crumpled, sweaty twenty-dollar bills.

"Welcome to…" the pimply boy behind the counter began in a flat voice, long since tired of repeating the same phrase.

"Sixty!" Andy barked and slammed the money down on the counter. Something thick and sticky pasted the money to the counter.

"Sixty?" the boy asked. "Um, we don't have a number sixty meal. Sorry, dude."

"Sixty cheeseburgers," Andy clarified. "Now!"

"Seriously bro?" the boy scoffed. "That's a lot of crumbled cow meat, man."

"Now! Now! Now!" Andy yelled. He banged his fist with each word. Every hit sprayed slimy pink goo out onto the counter. Andy raised his fist, turning it slowly. Small rosy dots of gelatinous liquid dotted Andy's skin, weeping from Andy's pores.

"Might take a few minutes, man," the boy said with a disgusted smile as he peeled the tacky bills from the countertop. A thin string of a pink snot-like substance stretched from the bills before snapping and splattering the boy's face.

"Get. My. Food," Andy growled.

"Oh, come on," the boy gagged as he tried to rub the gluey substance from his face. "That's nasty, man. Jeez." He turned and pushed the microphone near his register. "Sixty cheeseburgers," he called in Andy's order, then added, "and send someone up front to clean off the counter."

Andy waited at the end of the counter as three sacks of 99-cent cheeseburgers were brought out to him. He had wanted a strawberry shake and fries, but found himself with no desire to consume either. All Andy could think about eating was beef.

Small beads of pink sweat peppered Andy's brow as he plopped down into his usual spot.

"Starve a cold," Andy whipped his hand across his forehead, smearing the liquid. He felt warm, maybe a little feverish. "Feed a fever," Andy smiled as he tore the paper wrapper off the first cheeseburger. It vanished in a matter of seconds. "One down, fifty nine to go."

Somewhere deep inside of Andy, the deafening chorus of tiny voices roared with approval, urging Andy to eat faster.

-16-

Kristen was hungry. Granted she was hungry on most days, what with all the dieting and workouts, but this hunger was different than the pangs she felt on her daily 400-calorie diet. This hunger couldn't be ignored.

Kristen rummaged through the cabinets and refrigerator desperate to find something that would take the edge off of her hunger, anything. She couldn't help but marvel at the fact that she would have any appetite, let alone feel ravenous, after the afternoon she'd had at the Jock Itch.

That, that...loser! That fat loser had vomited on her. Sure, there had been a phase with Kristen's second husband where they had 'experimented' and done things she would rather forget, but Roger had been a wealthy plastic surgeon, not an overweight shoe salesman. Roger's money could make a lot things seem less disgusting, even bedroom puke.

But upchuck or not, Kristen couldn't deny that she was hungry. No, not hungry, she was starving. Nothing helped. Nothing quelled the pangs roiling through her gut in fiery acidic waves.

"All this diet, health SHIT!" Kristen growled as she wrenched a cabinet door from its hinges. She was momentarily angry with herself for having ripped down the door, but also equally impressed. *All those Booty Boot Camps are really beginning to pay off!* Kristen dropped the cabinet door onto the tile floor with a hollow *thunk* and moved on to the next one. A thick string of pinkish gunk followed the door to the floor. Kristen was too hungry to notice.

Protein powder, dehydrated super greens, raspberry ketones, green coffee extract. All the crap fake doctors with daytime televisions had instructed her to purchase to shave years off her look. All the crap that had failed and nothing that Kristen wanted right   now.
"I want a..." Kristen thought for a second. "I want a freaking triple bacon cheeseburger with fries! That's what I want!" She hadn't eaten fast food for years, refusing to waste the calories or to be

seen in such a place. But right now, it was all Kristen could think about.

"I'll go through the drive thru," Kristen reasoned with herself as she grabbed her purse and keys. Slimy pink handprints covered her kitchen table. "No one will see me that way. And tomorrow I'll do a double in spin class. No harm, no foul."

Kristen started her car with the remote and flopped down into the seat, perhaps a bit harder than she intended to. A wet *squish* tumbled through her yoga pants in an unsettling wave. "Seriously?" Kristen whimpered, but quickly growing angry at delaying her obtaining of charred cow flesh. "Did I seriously just crap my pants?"

Trembling hands pulled at the waistband of the Kristen's yoga pants before searching for the source of the offending *squish*. Something was definitely wet, tacky and disgusting in Kristen's yoga pants.

"Great," she groaned. "This will probably stain the leather. The perfect end to a perfect day." Kristen pulled her hands free, expecting to find them coated with brown. Her hands were pink. Covered with a hot pink, gluey substance. The same substance that loser Andy had vomited all over her earlier today.

Kristen wanted to scream, run into her condo and shower. She found herself shifting her car into drive and backing out of her carport. No one in the drive thru would be able to see the mess she had just created. Her foot stomped down on the down on the gas pedal causing a frothing pink torrent to erupt from both sides of her running shoe. Pink diarrhea, be damned, Kristen wanted a bacon cheeseburger.

-17-

"Damn it!" Squirrel yelled as he stepped down on another bottle cap. That was the third one so far. "How does every damn bottle cap end up on that side?"

Guy had dropped Squirrel off a good three miles outside of town, which normally wouldn't have bothered him much, but with only one sandal, Squirrel was finding it excruciating.

"As if pink slime and aliens and government cover ups weren't bad enough," Squirrel groaned. "No, let's just make it a tiny bit worse by dropping the one human who actually wants to stop this extraterrestrial crap from destroying the Earth, oh I dunno? Maybe three miles outside of town with only one god damn sandal?" Squirrel shook his fist at the sky hoping that Guy saw.

The truth was that Squirrel was relieved to have been dropped so far outside of town. It gave him time to think, but no good ideas came to mind. Running seemed like a good one, but how could he abandon Andy? Andy was his only friend and had become infested with some sort of alien garbage slime. He needed Squirrel's help. But how was he going to get through to Andy? It was hard enough when there wasn't freaking aliens and actual pink slime involved. Now it felt like it was going to be impossible to get Andy to stop eating the crap.

A car whizzed past Squirrel, a cloud of grit and dust rolling close behind.

"Sure, don't stop," Squirrel coughed as he waved his middle finger. "Just a kid walking alone on a dark road at night with ONLY ONE DAMN SANDAL!" At that moment, Squirrel would have given anything to be in Andy's basement killing the brain cells that remembered the day.

A dented panel van rumbled past and then slowly rolled to a stop a few yards away from Squirrel. The van had one right headlight and was covered with more rust than paint. As Squirrel got closer, he saw that the rear bumper was held in place with an assortment of both duct and packing tapes.

"Y'all need a ride 'der lil' man?" the driver barked from where he leaned out the driver's side window. Squirrel could see that the driver wore no shirt and had on overalls. Tufts of orangey hair stuck out from either side of a sweat stained Miami Dolphins hat.

"Sure," Squirrel called back. Might as well add getting molested to the list of ways the past few hours have been terrible.

"Where ya' goin'?" the driver asked as Squirrel climbed into the van. The dashboard was covered with a myriad of sun bleached Beanie Babies. A yellowed unicorn with a glittery gold horn coyly smiled at Squirrel as if it knew something he didn't.

"Into town, please," Squirrel replied, as he noticed that the passenger side door handle was missing. "I've got to see a man about a cheeseburger."

-18-

Halfway through his cheeseburger binge, Andy looked up to see Cece coming into the restaurant through the grimy doors. She must have been coming in for the late shift. She was in her usual fast food drone attire, but Andy found himself drawn to her. He had always thought Cece was beautiful, but he wasn't the kind of guy she'd date. Andy knew he wasn't the kind of guy any girl would date. But at that moment, none of those thoughts seemed to matter to Andy. He was charged up and felt like anything was possible. Maybe it was the cheeseburgers or maybe it was the fact that he had puked on two people that he really hated? Either way, Andy found himself weaving around screaming snot nosed children as he moved to intercept Cece.

"Hey! Cece! Hey!" Andy called out. His voice sounded weird, a little garbled. Probably still fighting off that bug or whatever. No matter, though, Cece had heard him.

"Oh, hey, Andy," Cece smiled. "No ducks today?"

"Nope," Andy said without a note of embarrassment. "That's my weekend uniform. New rule at the Jock Itch. Saturdays mean a crack full of ducks."

Cece laughed. "It's a good rule. Maybe I should drop that one in the suggestion box? My last suggestion didn't go over so well." Cece shrugged and looked behind the counter. Her manager was busy convincing some horrible woman and her toddler, the size of a twelve year old, that all of the chicken nuggets came with chewy, hard bits in them. Of course, it wasn't a beak or toenail.

"Oh yeah? What was your last suggestion?" Andy asked.

"That my manager Dale stick his head in the Fry-A-Lator and see how long he could hold his breath," Cece grinned. "I'm pretty sure he knows it was me, because he's been a total dick since I wrote it."

"How would he know?" Andy asked, feeling a sudden urge to hold Dale's head down in the fry oil.

"I dunno," Cece shrugged. "Maybe he recognized the handwriting? Or maybe it was because I signed it?" A quick burst of stifled laughter shook Cece's shoulders. Andy was intoxicated by her laugh. She was more beautiful than he had even realized.

"So, Cece," Andy began. Anything was possible today. He would ask her out and she would say yes, Andy could just feel it. Before he finished asking the question, Dale's high-pitched voice screeched across the restaurant.

"Cece, get to your station now!" Dale shrieked. "Right now!"

"Sorry, Andy," Cece smiled sadly. She knew he was going to ask her out. Was she saying sorry about Dale or sorry that she didn't want to go out? "We'll talk later, okay? Like maybe Friday night?" She smiled again, but this time, the glimmer was back in her eyes.

Andy's heart thudded in his chest and for once, it wasn't for cheeseburger related reasons. He actually had a chance with Cece! She had only hinted at it, but Andy knew. Today was the day his life turned a corner.

"Right now, Cece!" Dale shouted, his voice cracking as it went even higher. He was headed towards Andy and Cece.

"I had better go," Cece said, but it was too late. Dale was already there.

"I don't pay you to make love connections. I pay you to sell cheeseburgers," Dale snapped. "Though I guess it's one in the same in this situation, huh?"

"Shut up, Dale," Cece growled as she pushed past him.

"What's that you said, Cece?" Dale smirked. "It sounded like you said that you were volunteering to go unclog the backed up crapper in the men's room. That's so nice of you. Such a team player."

Cece sighed. "Whatever, Dale."

"Oh, the plunger?" Dale laughed. "Yeah, it's back there by the mop, but the handle broke so you're really going to have to get down in there. Thanks so much, Cece."

Andy had heard and seen enough. Something snapped. His fingers balled into two large hammy fists.

"You really should be nicer to Cece," Andy's voice rumbled like was birthed in thunderheads.

"And why's that?" Dale scoffed. "Is her knight in flabby armor going to defend his lady's honor? Because I'll tell you what, Sir Eats-A-Lot, that little princess doesn't have much honor left to defend. Just ask half the guys that work here."

"Apologize," Andy spat through gritted teeth. It was one word, but it carried countless unnamed threats. Dale took a step backwards, bumping into the condiment station.

"Hey look," Dale said holding his hands up. "I was just kidding, okay? I'm sure she's a wonderful girl."

Andy relaxed slightly.

"She'd have to be a saint to let you give her the ol' chub rub," Dale murmured out the side of his mouth as he started to walk away. "Or she must really like bean bag chairs."

Andy's hand shot out at a speed that even seemed to shock him. His fingers closed around the collar of Dale's manager's uniform like a steel vice. In a wide sweeping arc, Andy brought Dale crashing down onto the top of the condiment station. Packets of ketchup, mustard and mayonnaise burst under Dale's body as it smashed down.

Dale opened his mouth to scream, but Andy loomed over him, his own mouth open. A torrent of pink vomit spewed forth, hot and frothing, covering Dale's face and filling his mouth. After the gush of strangely colored puke dribbled to a stop, Andy let Dale fall to the floor. The manager was silent, unmoving, but breathing. Andy dragged the back of his hand across his face and spat a little remaining puke onto Dale.

Everyone in the restaurant watched the events unfold with a silent fascination, as if everyone other than Andy and Dale had frozen in time. Cheeseburgers were held midair, the most recent bite remaining only half chewed in the gaping mouths of onlookers. Fistfuls of fries had frozen, suspended motionless in time.

As Andy looked up, the spell was broken. All at once, the customers began to panic and scream. People tripped over one another as they dove from their seats and ran for the doors. Now it was Andy's turn to watch with silent fascination.

"What did I do?" Andy asked himself. But the answer was already screaming from inside. The countless voices of Andy's interior chorus roared in response to his question. Dale deserved what happened. He had all but asked for it. All of these people had. Years of watching Andy, judging him, mocking him and why? Because they thought they were better than him? Because they had the magical white trash gene that allowed them to subsist on nothing but fast food and still stay skinny? No, these people were just as bad as Dale. Just as bad as Todd. They needed to learn a lesson. They needed to be punished.

The first of the fleeing customers rammed into the glass doors leading out of the restaurant, but was thrown back. The doors were chained shut. People began to crowd into the tight little glass box that formed the entryway. A loud ear splitting sound vibrated the glass as something was dragged across the outside. Everyone inside fell silent.

A wide smear of thick pink goo slowly dripped across the glass.

"Something is out there," a lady with bleached hair and bad roots said as she pressed her face against the glass.

WHAP! WHAP! WHAP! A skeletal hand suspended in pink slime beat against the glass. The rest of the monster loped from the shadowy bushes near the left of the entrance. A toothy grin stretched across the creature's skeletal face. The rest of its body was vaguely human in outline, but almost completely shapeless. Thick ropes of pink gel hung, swinging lazily with the monster's stilted movements. In the center of the mass of slime, a human skeleton, intestines and organs could be seen floating. The skeleton raised its arm, again smashing it against the glass.

Wide, web like cracks spread across the glass like the work of thousands of tiny spiders. The pink slime quickly filled the cracks, seeping into the entrance and further breaking the glass.

"Run!" Someone screamed as everyone spilled out of the main entrance and back into the restaurant. One by one, people reported the same thing. All the doors were chained shut.

"We can climb out the drive thru window!" another customer offered. People leapt over the counter, heading for the small sliding window. The creature outside continued to press against the glass.

As the first customer climbed onto the small counter in front of the drive thru window, an explosion buckled the wall inward and threw the entire restaurant into darkness. The customer was thrown headlong, crashing into a life-sized fiberglass model of the chain's nightmarish mascot. A dark line of red ran down the clown's fiberglass face, becoming lost in its cheery cherry lipstick smile. The customer lay at its oversized feet, as if in a plea for mercy.

The front end of a car peeked through the wall where the drive thru had only moments before stood. People groaned and cried out in gloom. A few emergency lights cut into the darkness, but nothing was easily seen. Only dark shadows and shapes moved in the restaurant.

Andy stood motionless. Something inside told him that he would be okay. In fact, in just a little while, Andy would be even better than okay. This was the day that Andy's life turned that corner. This was the day that Andy made everyone who had ever made fun of him realize the mistake they had made. Andy was going to get even today. All he had to do was wait.

A second creature appeared outside the ruined drive thru window. It let out a gargled cry and began forcing its way inside the restaurant. There was no way to keep it out. The car had opened up too many spaces in the wall.

"They're inside!" someone screamed.

Others screamed out as well. Their words were lost under the chorus of breaking glass and burbling growls that soon filled the restaurant.

A thin smile stretched across Andy's face. All he had to do was wait.

-19-

"Looks like yer gonna haft ta git dat burger somewheres else ma' friend," the driver of the van said to Squirrel as they rolled into the parking lot. The restaurant was dark, but Squirrel thought that he could see movement inside.

"You might be right, Charles," Squirrel nodded as he rolled down the window and opened the passenger side door from the outside.

Charles, it turned out, was something of a self-proclaimed traveling preacher. The rear of the van was stocked with boxes of Bibles. Charles had memorized the entire book cover to cover. The three miles back into town wasn't really much of a drive, but filled with Charles's endless religiously themed prattling, the trip felt endless to Squirrel.

"Y'all make sure ta keep God in yer heart, Squirrel," Charles shouted as Squirrel walked towards the restaurant.

"Will do," Squirrel waved. *At least, I didn't get molested,* Squirrel thought to himself as he grabbed the front doors. A heavy chain was strung between the handles and locked. Ropey cords of pink goo dangled from the chain and handles. Some of the glass in the doors and windows had been smashed. The jagged edges were coated in the same pink ooze.

Something or someone thudded against the door leaving a greasy smear in its wake.

Somewhere in the darkness, a form shifted, momentarily passing through the light.

"Andy! Andy!" Squirrel shouted as he banged on the glass. More slime coated hands beat against the remaining panes of glass. Others grabbed for Squirrel through the broken windows. How the hell was Andy in there with those things?

"Oh man," Squirrel muttered. "This is bad, really bad." More and more of the pink slime covered things were amassing near the doors.

"Run, Squirrel," Cece yelled as she tore around the side of the restaurant.

"Cece?" Squirrel muttered.

"CECEEEE," a voice boomed from inside the darkened restaurant. It was monstrous and inhuman, yet something about the voice reminded Squirrel of Andy.

Cece sprinted past Squirrel and ran straight towards Charles's van. Four things followed close behind Cece. They were human or at least had been, but now were little more than mobile piles of slime with a skeleton suspended in the middle. Squirrel had seen enough and turned to follow Cece.

"What the hell is going on?" Squirrel shouted. "Where's Andy?"

"In there!" Cece cried as she fumbled with the passenger side door handle.

"Wait!" Squirrel yelled. "We can't leave him in there with those things!"

"Squirrel," Cece yelled back, "Andy *is* those things!"

Cece got the door open and pulled herself up into the van. Squirrel tore across the parking lot. Charles appeared shocked by the entire situation and sat dumbfounded in the driver's seat.

"Charles!" Squirrel screamed. "Snap out of it, man! Drive! Drive the god damn van right now!"

"Taint no need ta take der Lord's name in vain, son," Charles muttered from his stupor.

"If there ever was a time to do that, it's right now!" Squirrel grunted as he leapt into Cece's lap and slammed the door.

Charles opened his mouth to debate Squirrel, but a large gooey hand crashed through the window, forcing its fingers into Charles's mouth. The skin beneath the touch of creature immediately began to bubble and disintegrate. Charles screamed and flailed, but the pink slimy fingers bore deeper and deeper into his flesh.

"Get out! Get out! Get out!" Cece shrieked as she pushed Squirrel off her. A creature slammed into the passenger door.

"I can't," Squirrel said sadly. "The door only opens from the outside. I'm not rolling that window down."

Charles stopped moving. His skin sizzled and popped, filling the cab of the van with the unsettling aroma of burnt human flesh. His body was wrenched through the window of the van. A loud thud sounded outside the van as Charles's body tumbled into the parking lot. The sizzle and reek of burnt flesh intensified as the creature collapsed onto Charles, absorbing his body into its own.

"What now?" Cece yelled as scrambled into the back of the van. "He had the keys!"

"Give me a box!" Squirrel demanded. "Keep sending them up here!"

Cece began handing the heavy boxes of Bibles to Squirrel, who in turn piled them in front broken window. Squirrel moved into the back of the van, pushing the final box in place. They had filled the entire cab of the van, but knew it wouldn't hold for long.

"That's not going to last long," Cece said, her voice cracking. "Those things got through doors and windows, so a few boxes won't do much."

"It's better than nothing," Squirrel protested. The boxes shifted and bulged back into the rear of the van. Pink slime slowly began seeping in through small spaces between the boxes.

"You were saying?" Cece groaned as more and more of the slime oozed into the back of the van.

-20-

Things were quickly spiraling out of control. Guy had been monitoring Andy and the activity in the fast food restaurant since he dropped Squirrel in the field. Guy hoped that Squirrel could get his friend to see reason, get Andy to stop consuming so much of the blight, but it was too late. It was more than too late. The situation unfolding beneath his craft was far worse than anything Guy or his people had imagined.

Models had shown that the blight could infect living organisms if enough of it was consumed, but it had been assumed that no one could ingest that quantity. Guy saw just how wrong they were. Humans were capable of degrees of gluttony well beyond what a computer simulation could comprehend. Humans were willing to ignore bodily signals and continue to consume food that was obviously toxic. Andy had done this to a degree that shocked Guy.

"How has he eaten this much?" Guy pondered as he zoomed his view. Through one of restaurant windows, Guy watched as Andy consumed a nauseating amount of charred beef flesh, all of it infected with the blight. Soon after, Guy watched as Andy picked a grown man up with one arm, slammed him into a counter and vomited blight all over the man.

"That is well beyond human capabilities," Guy worried. Andy shouldn't have been this strong and definitely shouldn't have been vomiting massive quantities of the blight onto some poor man.

Andy had filled his body with the blight. Had completely allowed it to overrun his system and change his physiology. Andy was beginning to mutate and so was the blight.

A strange pink creature appeared on the edge of the parking lot. It carried a long length of chain in its hands. This creature was something completely new. Guy's computer directories could not place this being. It was of no known planet or species.

The creature appeared to be covered with blight or almost completely made of it. Guy zoomed in on the creature and gasped as he observed a human skeleton, intestines and organs floating in the center of the mass of blight.

"It was a human," Guy announced to no one other than himself. How had a human changed into that thing? It had to have some connection to Andy. Why else would the creature be heading directly towards the restaurant?

No, not heading towards it, chaining and locking the doors. The creature was trying to keep people inside. Moments later, a car slammed into the side of the restaurant. A second creature emerged from the car and began forcing its way inside the restaurant.

A poorly maintained van rolled into the parking lot and Squirrel emerged from the passenger side. He was heading towards the restaurant, completely unaware of what waited inside.

"No, stop!" Guy cried. "Squirrel, don't go in there!" Guy wanted to stop Squirrel, wanted to help him, but that went against the rules his people enforced. They were allowed to make contact and advise, but not to interfere. The American government becomes very upset when aliens make their presence known, let alone use extraterrestrial technology on Earth. Guy was not allowed to help, but how could he watch his new friend die?

Squirrel and a human female ran from the restaurant. Four of the creatures pursued them back to the van. A third human, this one apparently the driver, was pulled out of the vehicle and consumed. The blight simply absorbed him, because that was what it had been designed to do.

The creatures began attacking the van. It was poorly kept and wouldn't last long under the creatures' attack. Guy needed to do something.

One of the creatures pushed its way into the van. It was going to kill and consume Squirrel. There were rules Guy was required to follow. There was protocol for operations on Earth, but it never addressed this situation. It never gave guidelines for this scenario. No one had ever even dreamt the blight could achieve this level of violence, infection and cognizance. It simply had not been designed to do this, yet it was.

"What is it that humans say?" Guy wondered. "Rules are made to be broken? Yes, that is it! And yes they are!" Guy decreased the altitude of his ship.

There would undoubtedly be repercussions for violating protocol, and for interfering. The American government would surely be angry, but it would pale in comparison to Guy's own people. Violating protocol and revealing yourself to large numbers of subjects would not be looked upon kindly. Guy would definitely face severe punishment.

Maybe it was from being alone or maybe it was the earthling's influence, but Guy did not care what the protocol stated. He was going to help.

-21-

Andy watched people panicking. Some part of him felt the urge to flee, to run alongside the others…well, okay to walk quickly alongside the others. But Andy remained rooted to the ground. His inner chorus had risen to deafening levels, commanding him to stay, and wait for what was to come.

The first creature and then the second burst into the restaurant. Dale flopped at Andy's feet, transforming into another of the monsters. Andy should have been afraid, terrified like everyone else, but he wasn't. Andy felt excited. He felt better than he could ever remember feeling.

The two creatures fell on the fleeing customers. Flesh sizzled and disintegrated as the pink slime oozed over them. With each consumed victim, the creatures grew larger. Dale, now a monster himself, rose from the floor and flung himself on a nearby man who cowered beneath a table.

Long smoky tendrils of melted flesh filled the air making things hazy and difficult for Andy to see what was going on. Still, Andy didn't feel afraid. The creatures weren't there to hurt him. No, they were there to right the wrongs done against him. They were there for him.

The three creatures, now substantially larger, circled around a group of trembling patrons. They moved in unison, corralling the people and moving them towards Andy.

"Help us," a woman whimpered. "Help us, please."

"Help you?" Andy mocked. "So now the butt of your jokes has become your only hope, huh? Zero to hero just like that?"

"What are you talking about?" the woman cried. "I don't even know who you are! Please just help us!"

"Don't even know me?" Andy repeated. "But that never stopped you, did it? Never stopped you for making fun of me, did it?"

"I already told you," the woman yelled, "I don't know you! I never said anything about you! I was just stopping here on my way through. I just needed the bathroom."

"The bathroom?" Andy asked. Some part of him appeared to hesitate. He didn't know this woman. In fact, he had never seen her before in his life.

But that won't stop her from making fun of you! She'd do it eventually! Get home and tell everyone about the lard ass she saw when she took a bathroom break! Probably even has a picture on her phone so she can laugh at you over and over and over again! Are you really going to let that happen, Andy? The chorus in Andy's head screamed.

"I'll help you," Andy smiled humorlessly as he held out his hand. His eyes were dark and clouded, but the woman reached for his hand anyway. Andy delicately took the woman's hand and helped her from the floor. "I'll help you see just what a mistake you made by making fun of ME!"

Andy wrenched the woman's hair back. She cried out in pain, her mouth going wide. Andy leaned towards her open mouth and released a gushing torrent of pink vomit. Thick, ropey strings of puke wrapped themselves around the woman's head. Her arms flailed helplessly as Andy filled her throat, nose and lungs with the slime. When her arms went limp, Andy dropped her to the floor.

Moving towards the remaining people, Andy smiled. These people who once mocked him, who made him feeling like less than nothing, they would be the ones that helped him teach this entire town of red-necked ignorant assholes a lesson. This would be Andy's army. The chorus in his head cheered and urged him forward.

The people cowering before Andy had two choices. Run and get absorbed by one of the slimy, bubbling monsters or wait for Andy to puke on them. One teenage boy made a break for it, dashing through an opening between two of the creatures.

"Eat him," Andy commanded.

One creature turned and released a tangled pink tentacle that wrapped around the boy's leg. The boy screamed in agony as slime began to eat into his leg. The tentacle dragged him back towards Andy. The boy was lifted off the ground, and dangled above the others. The slime burned through his flesh and muscle, finally reaching bone. The oily pink tentacle undulated with greasy ripples, bubbles perforating the surface as it dangled the teenager above the frightened onlookers. Spittle frothed at the edges of the boy's mouth while he mewled in agony. Smaller tentacles emerged from the larger one and peeled back the boy's skin before plunging into his muscle. The meat of the boy's leg bugled and popped as the slime ate its way through. The skin bubbled and turned gooey, raining down on the others.

"Pleeeeeaaaasssseeee," the boy whined.

Andy nodded and the tentacle whipped sideways, snapping the boy's leg bone with a sickening *crunch*. The boy fell into the center of the other patrons, spasms of pain racing across his wrecked body. Tendrils of steam wept from the jagged stump of his leg as the slime continued to eat its way into the ruined leg.

"Make it stop!" the boy screamed. "I'll do anything! Just make it stop!"

Andy surveyed the other people. They were scared. That was good.

"Open your mouths," Andy ordered. The people hesitated. "NOW!"

Mouths opened and eyes were squeezed shut, screwed tight and determined not to see the impending horror unfolding before them.

Andy smiled. Then he released a violent spray of vomit.

-22-

The van rocked back and forth as the slimy nightmares battered the outside of it. One was slowly working its way in through the shattered driver's side window as Squirrel and Cece were thrown around the now empty back area of the van. The boxes they had used to block the creatures outside pushed back towards them. Squirrel dove for the boxes in a heroic attempt to reinforce them, but Cece grabbed his sweatshirt and pulled him back.

"What?" Squirrel demanded.

"There's slime all over those boxes," Cece pointed to thin trails of pink goo that leaked between the boxes. "If you touch that, you're done. It'll eat right through you."

"Thanks," Squirrel nodded and backed a little further away from the boxes. "How'd you know that?"

"I saw it happen inside," Cece paused. "I saw them go after people that tried to run away. One of those…monsters shot out like a…a tentacle or something and grabbed a boy. It ate right through his leg and then snapped the bone. Andy just stood there, like he was proud or something."

"Why would Andy do that?" Squirrel argued. "No way he'd do that! He's not like that at all!"

"I didn't think so either," Cece added. "We had been talking and then my manager Dale was being a total jerk. Andy freaked out and slammed Dale into the condiment station and then puked all over him. It was the same pink crap those monsters are made of. I don't know how Andy did it, but he did. After I saw that, I snuck into the back. Things got really crazy inside before I snuck out."

"I can't believe that Andy would do that," Squirrel said. "Andy's not one of those macho agro assholes. That's just not him. No way, man. But Guy said the slime could alter him…"

"I know what I saw," Cece replied. "Wait, who the hell is Guy?"

"Look, a day ago, I would have said you were crazy," Squirrel sighed, "but I just spent the last few hours in a spaceship with an alien named Guy, so I guess anything is possible."

"Alien?" Cece asked. "Are you serious?"

"Long story," Squirrel said. "But Guy is here to help contain the pink slime. He thinks Andy is completely infected with it. I was on my way here to try to help him, but I was obviously too late."

The van was rocked up onto two wheels, throwing Cece and Squirrel against the bare metal walls. Cece yelped in pain as Squirrel landed on top of her.

"They're going to tip us," Cece cried. "Where the hell is that alien of yours now? I think we could really use his help right about now!"

A blinding blue light spilled in through the small porthole windows in the side of the van.

"What now?" Cece worried.

"I think it's Guy," Squirrel smiled.

The blue light wavered and then disappeared, completely leaving the inhabitants of the van in darkness once again. The creatures outside the van continued forcing their way into the vehicle.

"That's all?" Cece snapped. "Your alien has mastered space travel, but the most he can do to help us is a stupid blue light? Gee, how amazing and impressive. What a help that was! Next thing we know he'll..." Cece's words trailed off as a new light shone outside the van, this time red.

"Ouch!" Cece cried when her hand touched the side of the van. "That's freaking hot!" The van stopped moving.

The vibrant red light grew in intensity, changing to an almost amber hue. The plastic porthole windows in the sides of the van bubbled and began to melt. A disgusting smell permeated the interior of the van, leaking in from the outside. A sound similar to children crushing bubble wrap filled the air, making it impossible for Squirrel and Cece to talk. The two stayed in the middle of the van listening the sound.

The red light flickered and then turned back to the blinding blue beam. The rear doors of the van ripped off and were thrown across the parking lot. The light filled the interior of the van. Outside the van was silent, but screams and other horrifying noises drifted out of the darkened restaurant.

"What do we do now?" Cece asked.

"Jump into the light!" Squirrel shouted as he leapt from the rear of the van and was lifted into the air.

Cece hesitated, but followed close behind.

The two were carried upwards towards the hovering ship, no longer cloaked and in its full triangular shape. The mechanical squid maw opened to bring Cece and Squirrel inside the ship.

As Squirrel approached the opening, a deafening roar shook the night. A pink, burbling tentacle as thick as a telephone pole erupted from the roof of the restaurant. The tentacle flicked back and forth, glowing faintly in the jaundiced light of the restaurant's sign. A powerful ripple passed through the tentacle before it sprung forward and latched onto the corner of the triangular ship. It whipped the ship back and forth, shaking Squirrel and Cece violently, still suspended midair. With one last powerful undulation, the tentacle sent the ship, Squirrel and Cece spiraling through the cold night sky.

-23-

Cece and Squirrel were outside the restaurant, trapped in the back of an old beat up van. Andy knew this because the slime creatures knew this. He was connected to them. They were of him; a part of him and when they felt pain, Andy suddenly realized that he did as well.

The searing waves of excruciating pain radiated through Andy's body, a body that had grown substantially, swelling and bulging to unnatural proportions. Andy could feel more and more of the pink goo coursing through his body. It was a part of his body, yet he felt that it had its own identity and agenda. Whatever this stuff, this slime was, it had bonded with Andy's body and he liked it. He liked the power, the sense of control. All he had to do was let it take over. All in all, Andy figured that it wasn't much of a trade on his part. Surrendering the sad fragments of his life and the bloated body that he inhabited to the slime was a no brainer for the chance to get even with all of the people who had mistreated him.

Whatever that light was, it hurt. It superheated the air and destroyed the creatures, drying them out and leaving them as little more than crumpled piles of chalky pink dust and bone. The light had come from some strange triangular object that hovered thirty feet or so above the van. One of the creatures had momentarily looked up, seconds before it was cooked, giving Andy a glimpse of the ship. He had no idea what it was, who was piloting it or where it had come from, but he hated it. Andy hated the ship and whoever was in it more than he had ever hated anything in his entire life.

"CECEEE!!!" Andy's voice boomed from within restaurant, echoed by all of the slime monsters. This ship was going to try to take her away from him just when he had seen that there was a chance. Andy's anger, once smoldering and dangerous, burst into an uncontrollable rage, the flames consuming the small bits of Andy's humanity that struggled to survive.

There were no more patrons left inside the restaurant, all having been transformed or consumed. It was now filled with creatures, all burbling piles of pink slime, a wickedly grinning skeleton floating amongst a sea of organs in the middle each repulsive monster. Andy called out to them, beckoned them to join him, embrace him, and become one.

Moments later, a gigantic pink tentacle burst from the roof of the restaurant. Andy's mind, the slime's mind had been made up. Whatever this thing in the sky was, it was a threat and needed to be destroyed. If Squirrel and Cece were with this thing then they were a threat and needed to suffer the same fate. Everyone did.

-24-

Squirrel watched his feet change position with his head. Somewhere in the background, Cece screamed as she spun through the night sky.

Guy had managed to keep both securely within the blue light, but couldn't bring them into the ship. It was simply too dangerous with the ship spinning uncontrollably through the air. He only hoped that the two humans would be safe.

A sharp pain burst from the right side of Squirrel's head. Something warm and tacky filled his ear. He slowly moved his hand to his ear. Things felt slow, sounded off, as if Squirrel was moving at half speed. Granted, this feeling wasn't one that Squirrel was completely unaccustomed to, but this was still somehow different. Squirrel's hand came away from his ears. It was sticky. His brain struggled to fit together what was going on.

"What the hell?" Squirrel mumbled as he splayed his fingers before his face. Then it dawned on him – he wasn't moving anymore, not only was he not moving, but also he was no longer flying through the air. He was on the ground and his hand was slick with blood, blood from the side of his head and in his ear, his blood.

"Squirrel?" Cece coughed from somewhere behind a thicket of thorn bushes.

"Yeah," Squirrel groaned, struggling to his feet. "I'm here. You okay?" The question was stupid, but one people asked out of habit and a lack of options.

"No, not really," Cece winced as she picked her way out from behind the bushes. "I mean, we just watched your friend team up with some slime monsters and eat a restaurant full of people I knew. Oh, and on top of that, it all has something to do with aliens and cheeseburgers. So no, Squirrel, I'm not okay. I'm pretty damn far from okay!"

"Yeah, I know," Squirrel agreed as he offered Cece his hand to help her the last few steps. "Other than that, our day pretty much sucked, huh?"

"Glad to see you sense of humor remained intact," a strange voice called.

Cece turned to see a small gray alien moving closer. It was as if someone had brought a child's drawing to life – the eyes and head oversized, long gangly arms and fingers. Its skin glistened in the moonlight, giving the alien a wet appearance, but as it came closer, Cece could see it was not moisture, but a series of small iridescent scales that shone on the alien's skin.

"I am Guy," the alien said extending its delicate hand to Cece. She gently shook it.

"Guy?" Cece asked. "Strange name for an alien."

"Don't ask to hear his real name," Squirrel warned. "Trust me, Guy is much better."

"I am sorry that I was unable to bring you into my ship in time to escape," Guy apologized. "Though I am not sure we would have been able to. Remaining suspended in the blue force field is most likely the only reason you are currently alive and unharmed."

"Speak for yourself," Squirrel grimaced as he touched the back of his head. A large knot had formed with a cut in the middle that slowly wept blood, but most had clotted and the wound didn't look serious.

"Your species can tolerate a great deal more than that," Guy grinned. "Your resilience is one of your most admirable attributes, my friend. I am sure that you are strong enough to continue. You are truly a credit to your people."

"Gee, thanks, Guy," Squirrel nodded. "I'm sure your people are proud of you too."

"Would the two of you please just make out and get it over with?" Cece smirked. "I mean, I'm sure you become closer after a probing and all, but we kind of have more pressing issues than an intergalactic bromance."

"What is a bromance?" Guy asked, tilting his oversized head to look at Cece quizzically. "I am not familiar with this word."

"Slang," Squirrel waved his hand dismissively. "It's a stupid word. Don't worry about it."

"Ah, yes slang," Guy nodded. "Your kind is renown for its ability to create new, useless words. It was perhaps a mistake for my people to give you what you call the internet. That bit of technology seems to have accelerated the break down of your communication skills, which was not our intention or purpose. No, we most certainly did not give you that for the purpose of showcasing cats. But then again, you do have the amazing ability to find new and useless applications for technology, so perhaps it was unavoidable?" Guy shrugged, shook his head and turned back to where his ship had crashed.

"Can it fly?" Squirrel asked, looking at the ship. It was partially buried, its cloaking device flickering sporadically. Squirrel felt the answer to his question was fairly obvious, but still needed to ask.

"Yeah," Cece added. "Let's get in that thing and go fry those slimy bastards with that red ray gun thing."

"A good idea indeed," Guy agreed, "but I am afraid my ship is in need of repairs and currently will not fly."

"Fry them?" Squirrel snapped. "Look, I'm all for killing those pink skeleton things, but we can't fry Andy. I mean, it's Andy. Cece you can't seriously think that frying Andy is the answer to this."

"I'm sorry, Squirrel," Cece said softly. Tears glistened in the corners of her eyes. "You didn't see what I saw inside that restaurant. It's not Andy anymore. I'm so sorry, but it just isn't. We have to stop whatever this is before it gets any worse."

"I couldn't agree with you more," a voice called from near the ship. It carried wintery notes of violence.

Guy, Squirrel and Cece snapped their heads around to see a man in an expensive tailored black suit walking around the side of Guy's ship. The man held a .45 caliber pistol, but had it at his side as if he didn't really expect to have to use it.

"Who the hell are you?" Squirrel demanded.

"In good time," the man grinned. "Assuming of course, that the three of you behave."

Four Black Hawk helicopters crested the tops of the trees. Blinding spotlights illuminated the small clearing. Thick ropes dropped from the sides, followed closely behind by heavily armed soldiers in black fatigues.

"Shit," Squirrel groaned as he stared at the helicopters. His parents' paranoia had more than schooled Squirrel in the meaning of unmarked black helicopters.

"Yes," Guy nodded, his lipless mouth pulled into a thin line. "I do believe that shit is the proper word to describe the situation in which we currently find ourselves."

-25-

Having been cut from a pure, Middle America corn-fed cloth, Agent Travis Howard was born to be an agency man. He had wanted nothing else for his entire life. While some boys dreamt of putting on a fireman's hat or tying a polished pair of soldier's boots, young Travis had spent days in his backyard flipping open one of his father's old wallets and pretending to be a federal agent.

After studying forensic accounting, Travis had been recruited by the FBI. He really had no desire to be an accountant, never planned on actually using the degree, but had remembered that it was a desirable background for a federal agent to have. It was strange that the FBI used financial means to bring down most criminals and surely wasn't what Travis was preparing for while he chased his dog around the backyard with a cap gun, but that was the reality of the job. Not everyone got to chase the bad guys. After a few years, Travis felt that young boy longing for adventure begin to whither and die. He made the decision to leave the agency.

When Travis handed his letter of resignation to the bureau chief, he expected him to be disappointed, to try to talk him out of his decision. He sure as hell didn't expect him to smile.

"You're ready," the chief had smiled.

"Ready?" Travis asked.

"For a promotion," the chief nodded.

"I don't think you understand," Travis clarified. "I'm here to quit. I can't take sitting at a desk looking over Caribbean bank statements for another day. I just can't do it anymore."

"That's never what you were recruited to do in the first place," the chief grinned. "We just had to make sure that you had the gumption to do something else. That you really wanted something more."

Travis didn't know what to say, so he agreed. What the chief described sounded exactly like what young Travis had dreamt of – journeying around the world, pursing the most dangerous criminals and crimes. That was what a real agent did, not that desk jockey bullshit he had wasted four years on.

Three days later, Travis had reported to Quantico. His life had never been the same and in the years to come, he would often wonder if he had made the right choice. Was chasing freaking aliens really what he had wanted to do? Then again, what kid didn't dream of battling aliens and saving the planet?

However, once again, the realities of the job were far from the action of his dreams. Sure, Travis got to know things that most people chalked up to the ramblings of bored hillbillies and lunatics. He got to see things that few other people ever would, but much like the criminals he had once pursued, dealing with aliens mostly meant paperwork.

It was true that Travis wore an expensive black suit, but he was definitely not on the set of Men in Black. There was no Will Smith or Tommy Lee Jones. There was no talking dog with a dirty sense of humor. None of Hollywood's misconceived notions greeted Travis as he walked through the doors every morning. What would undoubtedly be there was another mountainous pile of paper that no matter how much he got filed and stamped, would be larger the following morning. Aliens or not, Travis's job was riddled with just as much bureaucratic bullshit as any other government position.

The extraterrestrials were extremely careful and rarely conducted operations on Earth. Careful protocols had been worked out with the US Government and the aliens were in no rush to piss off what was widely accepted as the most aggressive and self-destructive race in the universe.

More times than not, Travis found himself simply observing an operation or periodic abduction to ensure that it followed proper procedure. Then he would be given a new bit of alien technology and have to fill out a mountain of paperwork before going back to pretending that nothing had ever happened and that none of these things existed. Travis often wondered if the iPod and cell phones were really worth a couple of rednecks and cows, but that was how his superiors wanted to run operations and Travis knew better than to question. Nevertheless, he was still bored.

The boredom lasted for five years. Then two days ago, a rouge ship entered US air space. It was cloaked, but still left telltale chemical trails in the sky that could be detected. Once the ship crashed, satellites triangulated its position and Travis found himself in the back of a large, unmarked Black Hawk helicopter headed for some town that hardly warranted naming on a road map.

What bothered Travis about the situation was the fact that no one in the agency or any of those typically in the know had any idea why the ship had arrived unannounced. This was highly unlikely and surely harkened to something serious. The aliens would never run black ops on Earth unless there was something major going down. And major with the aliens was always bad.

The aliens had trusted the agency to handle the recovery of the rogue battle droid that had been masquerading as Rosie O'Donnell. They had even trusted them to handle the time a particularly virulent strain of herpes had been spread through Hollywood courtesy of a rather promiscuous alien with a blond wig and a propensity for pretending to be a socialite and heiress. No, whatever was going on, it was bad, like end of the Earth bad.

The helicopters dropped Travis a few hundred yards away from the crash site. He wanted to walk in, assess the situation and then show the big guns. Whatever this situation was, it needed to be tactfully handled, but also with enough of a show of force to let the aliens know that the agency meant business.

Travis had expected heavily armed alien storm troopers. He had not expected a lone alien, a blonde girl in a fast food uniform and a slightly stoned neo-hippy.

"Call in the helicopters," Travis barked into his radio. This was unexpected and that could only mean bad things.

Slowly, it began to dawn on Travis that whatever horrible scenario he had thought was going on was worse – far, far worse.

-26-

Andy felt good, felt whole. He called the others to him, joined with them and become one. Andy finally felt like he belonged. A lifetime of being an outsider, a joke, had finally come to an end. He found his place, and even better, he found power.

The walls of the restaurant rattled, the mortar cracking and falling away as the slime forced its way between the bricks. The restaurant shifted, its roof sloping downwards at a dangerous angle. A section broke loose, shooting forward and toppling the now darkened sign.

A massive shadow spilled from the side of the restaurant. It stretched and pulled, inching forward like a meth-addled slug. A dried brown path of crumbly dead grass was left in the wake of the creature. Anything organic that the creature touched was drained of its life and was left as little more than a husk.

High from the absorption of so much energy the creature shifted its interior, moving bones and organs towards the center, towards Andy. The bones pulled apart and reassembled into a large morbidly ornate throne. Organs quickly wrapped around the bones, providing stability and cushion. The pink slime gently pushed Andy towards the throne. It was a gift to him, a physical representation of his importance. None of this would have been possible without Andy.

Andy allowed himself to be placed in the throne. It was comfortable, more comfortable than any chair he had ever forced his girth into. This was his throne, what he had waited for his entire life. Sitting in the throne, Andy waited for what was to happen next. The interior chorus sang for him to remain calm, and remain a part of it all. Slim tendrils of slime tried to slip into Andy's eyes, nose, mouth and ears. Panic momentarily flared in Andy's head as he worried that he might drown, but the chorus called out to him, demanded that he remain calm and assured Andy that all he had to do was allow the tendrils to do what they needed.

Just let us do what we need to do, what you want to do!

Andy held his breath. His lungs burned like they were suddenly filled with acid. Then Andy inhaled deeply. The slime, already in his gut raced through the rest of Andy's body. It connected to his brain, muscles and bones. It became Andy and he became it. The two were indecipherable from one another. Consuming it had allowed the slime to take over Andy's systems, but the new tendrils also gave him control, hardwired him to the entire creature. It was now one whole, essentially one giant cell, with Andy as its nucleus.

From his newly formed control center, Andy forced his thoughts outward. The slime pulled and began moving towards the center of town. It towered over the rows of one-story Mom and Pop shops that dotted Main Street, growing larger with each new meal. Soon it would surpass even the few two-story and three-story buildings that had popped up throughout town.

Looking out over the town, Andy's anger burned with a new intensity, having found a kindred spirit with which to share it. Andy was going to destroy it all. He was going to feed them all to the slime and leave not one building standing. Bones and bricks are all that would remain.

-27-

Squirrel watched the well-dressed man walk towards them. He held a gun, but only loosely at his side – there appeared to be little threat in his mannerisms.

"You know, this wasn't a sanctioned operation," the man in the suit yelled over the *thrum thrum thrum* of the four helicopters. "You didn't have clearance to land here. Protocol exists for a reason. There are steps," the man paused. "There's paperwork that has to be filled out and filed." He said the last part with an obvious note of disgust.

Squirrel and Cece stood frozen as soldiers, clad head to toe in black fatigues, unloaded from the helicopters. A few other people in civilian clothes followed closely behind the soldiers. They held strange instruments and appeared to be taking readings.

"Scientists?" Cece whispered.

"Government ones," Squirrel added with a shudder. His parents had warned him of people like these. While most parents worried about lusty old men roaming the streets with panel vans and pockets heavy with candy, Squirrel's had filled his head with nightmares of black government helicopters and strange scientists. It now appeared that their paranoia had not been completely misplaced.

Guy stepped forward. "There was no time for that, agent. Your paperwork is far less important compared to what I have come here to accomplish."

"It's not my paperwork," the agent sulked. "And it's Agent Howard. You came alone?" The agent's gun rose ever so slightly. "You never come alone. You have rules that demand teams of at least three or four."

"Yes, that is true," Guy nodded. "I came alone so as to avoid detection, but it appears that I have not succeeded in those regards."

"What did you come to do?" Agent Howard demanded.

"I have come to deal with the blight and the problem it poses," Guy answered honestly.

"The blight?" Agent Howard repeated. "You mean pink slime? What do you care about some crappy beef derivative?"

"Because, as my people told your government, it was not designed to be used in that manner," Guy replied. "We assumed that it would be safe if you used it to bolster beef supplies and feed those who do not have enough food. Those people would never consume enough of the blight to make it dangerous. Instead, you chose to add it to fast food and create an entire race of people that are addicted to it! Things have spiraled out of control!"

Squirrel was shocked to see Guy showing emotion. Up until this point, the little gray alien had been rather deadpan, only cracking a sly smile occasionally. Whatever was going on and whoever this agent was it appeared to really be bothering Guy.

"Things have changed," Agent Howard said.

"Yes, that is favorite line of your government," Guy sighed.

"Of course, it is," Squirrel snapped. "You're telling us nothing but lies. So with all due respect, Agent Howard, you can shove your whole g-man routine right up your butt. Guy's right and we're going to help him."

"Perhaps you are," Agent Howard admitted. "Perhaps you'll help him more than you even thought was possible." He raised his gun and motioned towards one of the helicopters. "Get in, all three of you."

-28-

Walter Kinsey was little more than a shadow in town. Sure there had been a time when he was All State and set records in both football and wrestling. He had his pick of the cheerleaders and barely had to work to get a passing grade in class.

Those glorious days were now little more than wrinkled, sepia toned memories that only mattered to Walter. Some hot shot Mexican kid had broken his record for rushing yards three years ago and just last year, some wiry little turd had destroyed his record for most wins on the mat. Walter's place in history, it seemed, was destined to be second place. Of course, that was assuming no one else surpassed him, which was most likely going to happen.

"All those border jumpers," Walter slurred as he sucked down two thirds of his eleventh Bud. "Them freaking border jumpers are ruining my records as well as this country. Coming over here with super endurance from running from the Border Patrol and whatnot. Shee-it, if it weren't for them, I'd still be number one! Number one!" He slammed his beer down on the bar, throwing a wide ring of foam. No one else in the bar was listening, but that never stopped Walter. His tireless recounting of high school sports stats and ignorant ramblings were just background noise, no more important than the Top 40 crap that droned out of the jukebox.

"I'll tell you what," Walter continued. "What we need is a disaster. Something to clean this damn town out, like a good flood or hurricane or something. That'd be something to watch. All them little turds trying to outrun a tidal wave instead of La Migra." Walter snorted and a jet of beer spewed from his nose.

No one paid attention. No one cared. That's what hurt Walter more than anything. He used to command the attention of the entire town. He was admired by his teammates and feared by other teams.

Now, he hardly garnered a second look. He was little more than a doughy racist shadow, drunkenly drifting through town in a stained varsity jacket that was now two sizes too small.

"Hey!" Walter shouted at the girl behind the bar. "Hey, skank! How'd you like to know what it's like to get it on with a sports hero?"

"Why?" she sneered. "You know where one is hiding in this hole?"

"F-ing lesbians," Walter grunted.

"What'd you say?" the girl retorted. "Best watch your mouth, Walter. I'll have my girlfriend take you outside and kick your ass."

Walter waved his hand dismissively. Maybe she was a lesbian? Maybe she wasn't? In the end, did it really matter? The girl saw him as a joke. Peeking at eighteen was a bitter pill to swallow - a pill that was most easily swallowed with whiskey.

"Gimme a shot of Jack!" Walter bellowed.

Walter watched the girl shoot him a dirty look, but then turn to grab the bottle of whiskey. At least, he could still get a woman to do that for him.

The stool that Walter drunkenly tottered upon began to vibrate and shake. He grabbed the brass rail on the edge of the bar to steady himself, but could still feel the tremors.

"A few too many?" the bartender smirked as she dropped the shot of whiskey in front of Walter. Her face quickly lost all notes of humor as she too felt the vibrations rumbling through her boots. "What the hell?"

"Earthquake or something?" Walter offered as an explanation.

"Round here?" the bartender began to argue, but the rumbling grew louder and her words were lost.

Walter heard a sound like the roar of a passing train. Then the rear wall of the bar collapsed, burying three pool tables and the eight of the patrons standing near them.

A wave of molten pink goo spilled through the wreckage. People screamed and tried to run, but thick ropes of the slime shot forward and pulled them into the main burbling mass. The people disappeared into the goo with loud hisses and streams of steam. Skin and muscle liquefied, trailing off through the monster in dark twisting currents before disappearing. Bones and organs were pulled towards the center, as if guided by invisible fingers, and joined to a darkened center that slightly resembled a man.

Walter leapt over the bar as a pink tentacle whizzed past his head, shattering the rows of liquor and mirror that lined the back of the bar.

"Holy shit!" the bartender exclaimed. "What is that? How are we going to make…" A thick cord of acidic pink slime wrapped around her neck, crushing both her words and windpipe before lifting her high into the air and over the edge of the bar. Walter watched her disappear.

"Better you than me," he grunted as he edged his way further under the bar. An unseen hook that hung beneath the bar top snatched at Walter's head, peeling back a long strip of scalp. Blood spilled down Walter's face. He pawed at his eyes, trying to get his vision to clear and only succeeding in making it worse.

"Damn it! Damn it!" Walter hissed. He was completely unaware of the snake-like tentacle that silently slithered up behind him. A searing ring of pain clamped around Walter's ankle. He fell flat onto the sticky bar mat, pawing for something to hold onto before disappearing around the corner with one last curse.

Andy felt the emotions of each person seeping into him through the slime. He felt their fear, their hatred and love. Their hopes and dreams were now Andy's to own. He felt everything that they were and wanted more. The taste was delicious. It was everything that Andy had chased through each fast food binge and empty cheeseburger wrapper. It was delectable. Andy wanted more.

-29-

An old warehouse on the edge of town had been taken over by Agent Howard and his team. Men and woman in matching black fatigues or white lab coats buzzed about the space. Some were on guard, constantly checking and rechecking the perimeter of the warehouse, even though it was at least fifteen miles outside of town in the middle of an abandoned industrial complex.

The scientists crawled across the wreckage of Guy's ship like ants. They pulled at edges and angles, trying to find something to analyze, but every time they gripped a piece, it turned liquid and melted back into the ship's hull. Squirrel caught a faint smile flicker across Guy's face every time a scientist cursed in frustration and watched the silvery material slip through their fingers.

"How does it do that?" Agent Howard demanded. He had moved Squirrel, Cece and Guy into an area in the middle of the warehouse. Bright halogen lights lit the space, but they felt even brighter above the semi-circle of metal chairs that Agent Howard had set up.

"It is designed to do that," Guy stated plainly.

"I understand that," Agent Howard nodded. "Please clarify as to how it does it, not why."

"That is not technology that I am allowed to share at this time," Guy shrugged. "I am sorry, but as you stated earlier, Agent Howard, there is protocol that must be followed. The design and workings of my ship are not currently open for discussion."

"Interesting that now protocol matters," Agent Howard smirked. "Now you're interested in following the rules, huh?"

"Why don't you just stop wasting all this time?" Cece interrupted. "Who knows what the slime is doing right now?"

"We'll get to that," Agent Howard dismissed her. "It will be handled."

"Get to it?" Squirrel barked. "And you'll handle it? Jeez, like how you handled the pink slime in the first place? It's no wonder that Guy won't tell you how his ship works. You'd just find some way to screw that up too!"

"Yeah, that's probably true," Agent Howard admitted. He appeared to deflate slightly. "We don't exactly have the best track record with new technology and the whole pink slime situation has spiraled out of control, which is regrettable."

"That is certainly one way to assess the current situation," Guy chimed in. He was evidently becoming more comfortable with sarcasm as well as emotion.

"Look," Agent Howard sighed, "I don't really give a crap if you tell me about the ship. My superiors told me I had to ask, but personally, I don't care. All of this alien bullshit and paperwork is getting old. All I really want to know is why you decided to come here alone and what that means for us."

"I had to," Guy answered. "My people are impeded by equally as many rules and barriers as you and your government. Similar to yourself, I find them problematic and exasperating."

"That doesn't mean that we don't follow them," Agent Howard grunted. "They exist for a reason."

"And sometimes, those reasons are not the right ones," Guy added. "Reasons and motivations are only valid if they help others."

Agent Howard opened his mouth to argue, but instead his mouth hung open as he considered what the alien had just said. He slowly closed his mouth and nodded.

"I knew that had I followed typical steps that I would have been denied permission," Guy continued. "So the decision was made to ignore those rules which had become obsolete. I commandeered a ship and charted it for Earth."

"You came here under your own direction?" Agent Howard almost laughed. "That's highly unusual for your people."

"True," Guy answered. "But sometimes what is unusual is what is most appropriate. Many of my people had decided that you had been warned about the blight, that we had instructed you as to how to use it properly and that you still chose to ignore them. You created the current disaster with what you call pink slime and therefore should have to clean it up. That is the opinion of many of my people, especially those who make decisions. I did not share their perspective, so I decided to try to assist."

"Okay," Agent Howard nodded slowly as he looked around the warehouse. No one appeared to be paying attention to Agent Howard or Guy. Aliens and interrogation was old hat to these people. "Look, let's take a break. Maybe get something to eat and clean up a bit? You guys look like you've been through hell. There are a few offices in the rear of the warehouse that have been modified to serve as bunkrooms. Showers are in the rear of each room. If you would like, I'll have someone deliver some clean clothes. I apologize that they will be jumpsuits, but that is all we currently have to offer."

"Jumpsuits?" Squirrel laughed. "Probably nice orange ones like they have Guantanamo Bay? Get us in those early and save some time?"

Agent Howard began laughing. "It honestly is all we have to offer, Mr. Moscovitz. I know that you and your parents have very little faith in your government, but we have no intention making you or Ms. Adams disappear."

"Squirrel, just call me that. Okay?" Squirrel responded. What Agent Howard had said was true, Squirrel didn't trust him, but on the other hand, the man did seem genuine, at least as genuine as a government drone could be.

"Okay, Squirrel," Agent Howard nodded. "Then please feel free to call me by my first name Travis. I promise you that I have no intention of seeing any harm befall any of you."

Cece, Guy and Squirrel shared a look and then nodded. They would trust Travis for the time being. It wasn't like they really had any other choice.

-30-

Sounds were muffled inside the slime, but Andy could still hear the screams of people as they were pulled into the mass. He savored each strained syllable. It was better than anything he had ever tasted. Every salty sweet morsel of fast food paled, seemed bland compared to the wonders that Andy found with each new victim.

The slime knew what Andy wanted and gave it to him. It could make him feel whatever he desired. The slime extended its tendrils into Andy's brain, massaged the folds and made sure he became more and more addicted to what it offered. The slime could function on its own, could move and eat, but it lacked the knowledge and imagination that Andy offered. It needed Andy's brain and ideas, so a strange symbiosis had been formed.

The chorus inside Andy's head fell silent, waiting for him to make a decision. Where would they go next? Who was next on the list?

"Everyone," Andy thought. "They all deserved to pay. Everyone was guilty."

What about your sister Rachel?

"No," Andy refused. "Rachel is annoying, but she always meant well. We leave her alone."

Everyone is guilty. Everyone hurt you, even her. She refused to accept you for who you were.

"Rachel loves me," Andy argued. "She's the only one that ever did!"

Loves you? A thin laugh echoed through the slime. *Is it love that allowed you to live in the basement? SHE IS EMBARRASED BY YOU! SHE HATES BEING YOUR SISTER! BEING THE SISTER OF THE TOWN JOKE! SHE WANTS YOU DEAD JUST LIKE YOUR MOTHER!*

"Shut up! Shut up! Shut up!" Andy shrieked.

Sorry, Andy. The chorus had returned to its usual soothing tone. *But you must recognize the realities of your world. It's harsh and unpleasant, but it must be done. Think about it, Andy, even if Rachel DID love you, could she still?*

"What the hell are you talking about," Andy demanded. "She's my sister. Of course, she could still love me."

Really? Do you really think so?

"What do you mean?" Andy questioned as he willed a tentacle to lash out. A police cruiser was tossed into the side of the post office building. The two officers screamed from inside the crushed cab. Thick lines of blood spilled down the dented door panel as an officer hung out the side. His face was mangled, but he somehow still managed to raise his pistol and unload a full magazine into the slime. Andy watched the bullets slow to a stop in the pink goo. The slime pushed the bullets out before sending a tentacle crashing through the shattered window of the police cruiser. The officers cried out in agony as their flesh wept from their bones in greasy red tears. After a few more screams, all that remained were two stained, goo-laden police uniforms.

Do you really think that Rachel COULD still love you after all that you have done? After what you've become?

"What I've become?" Andy whispered. For the first time since joining with the pink slime, Andy considered what he must look like. "I'm still me," he said weakly.

Of course you are, but you're so much more now. You've evolved. You've become something better than all the others in this town. They are weak. You are strong. The strong feast upon the weak. It is how your world works. Rachel is one of them. Rachel is food. The hungry can love food, but food cannot love the hungry. You must eat, Andy. WE MUST EAT!

Andy wanted to argue, but was suddenly distracted by a group of people in white lab coats. They hid in the shadows of a nearby alley and were trying to scrape samples of the pink slime into Petri dishes.

"Get them!" Andy bellowed, willing a massive wave of the slime forward. The lab coats vanished beneath the rosy tidal surge.

"Cece?" Andy muttered as he felt the lab coats' memories and emotions join the collective thoughts of the slime. She and Squirrel were with the alien and some government agent in a warehouse outside of town. "We're going to get Cece," Andy commanded. "I want Cece NOW!"

Of course, of course, Andy, but we have to take care of something else first.

"What is more important than what I want?" Andy screamed. "Cece is there and so is that freaking alien that took her! We need to get her and kill everyone else!"

Yes, we do and we will, but first, you have to fully commit to your new life, to OUR new life.

"What more can I do to show my commitment?" Andy growled. "Like there's anything left in my life to give you?"

Rachel. You have to cut all ties from your former life. You, no WE, have to join Rachel to us.

"You mean eat her," Andy clarified.

Think about your parents. They both abandoned you, Andy. Rachel will be one with us, with you forever. She will not be gone. She will be with you forever this way. This way, Rachel can never leave you Andy.

"I don't know," Andy hesitated.

How badly do you want Cece? How badly do you want what you truly deserve, Andy?

"Left at the next corner," Andy barked.

-31-

Andy should have been home by now, not that Rachel actually expected him to eat any of the food she had prepared for dinner. Every night, it was the same. She made something healthy, hoping against all odds, that Andy would come home and eat it. But every night, she at alone and Andy ate fast food.

A shadow moved past the kitchen window. Rachel looked up from where she was chopping vegetables for a salad. Why couldn't Andy at least try something she made? He might actually like it, but Rachel knew he never would. The crap he bought in the drive thru had reprogrammed his taste buds and appetite. Loving Andy was akin to having a drug addict in the family. He was completely strung out on greasy cheeseburgers and fries. Could you send someone to rehab for a fast food detox?

Another shadow, this one larger, moved past the window.

"What the heck is out there?" Rachel wondered out loud. She picked up the large bowl of salad and leaned towards the window.

The glass burst, flying inward and lacerating Rachel's face. She screamed in equal parts shock and pain as she tumbled backwards. Salad rained down around her. The thick wooden salad bowl flew backwards, knocking the simmering pot of vegetable stew off the stove.

Rachel screamed as the scalding liquid spilled off of the stove and poured over her head and shoulders. She leapt to her feet, still standing in a steaming pool of soup.

A burbling wave of pink goo spilled through the broken window. Tentacles shot forward, eagerly reaching for Rachel.

Shock rooted Rachel to her spot in the cooling pool of her would-be dinner. A tentacle grabbed her arm. It burnt the flesh, filling the kitchen with the reek of dissolved human muscle. Rachel immediately forgot about the pain caused by the soup burns. She swatted at the tentacle, but it had already recoiled, as if burned as well. Bits of the tentacle flaked and fluttered. Something outside of the house howled in anger.

Three more tentacles reached for Rachel, this time going lower, but recoiled the minute, they touched the puddle of soup.

94

Too scared to do anything else, Rachel remained standing in the pool of soup and salad.

A massive tentacle rolled through the window, buckling the wall and cracking the ceiling.

"RACHEEEELLLLLLLL!!!!" a hellish voice gurgled from somewhere outside.

"Andy?" Rachel said weakly. The house shook and rocked on its foundation. Jagged chunks of plaster rained down around Rachel. Dishes and pots spilled from the cabinets shattering on the floor.

Rachel looked up as half of the kitchen ceiling detached itself from the studs.

"Andy, what happened to you?" Rachel whispered before everything went dark.

-32-

Squirrel and Guy sat in one of the back rooms. Cece went into one of the adjacent rooms to try to wash away some of the memory of what happened inside the restaurant. Agent Howard, now just Travis, walked into Squirrel's room, pulled a chair into the center of it and sat down with a loud sigh.

"So you're serious when you say that you're rouge?" Travis asked looking at Guy. His prior façade of stone cold professionalism had melted away and been replaced with the image of a young man feeling old beyond his years.

"Yes, I guess you could phrase it that way," Guy nodded. He had climbed onto the top a desk. His spindly little legs dangled high above the ground and swung back and forth at a leisurely pace. Squirrel couldn't help but suddenly see the alien as a child.

"But what were you expecting to do?" Travis continued. "There wasn't much a lone alien and small ship could do."

"Perhaps, that is true," Guy shrugged. "But does that mean one should not try? I really did not have much of what you would call a plan."

"Great," Travis sighed acerbically. "That's just great."

"I'm sure he's open to suggestions, if you have any," Squirrel snapped. "It's real easy to sit there and be a pious government screw. It'd be a lot harder to actually offer something useful!"

"Fair point," Travis conceded. "It's just that, well, I guess I don't really know what to do either."

"Guy had a heat ray in his ship that fried those slimy pink nightmares," Squirrel offered. "Give him back his ship and let him have at it."

"I don't know that we could do that," Travis said honestly. "Too many people in the agency have an interest in his ship. The aliens never gave us access to one before, but since this wasn't sanctioned, we're free to tear it apart."

"You won't get inside the ship," Guy smirked. "Access to our ships is based upon genetic coding. It won't do anything for anyone other than myself."

"Figured as much," Travis nodded. "But what about that heat ray Squirrel was talking about?"

"It is no longer appropriate to employ that weapon," Guy said as he hoped down from the desk. He began pacing around the room, his iridescent scales shimmering under the harsh halogen lights.

"Why not?" Travis demanded. "Squirrel said that it cooked a few slime monsters. Why not use it on the main one?"

"Because Squirrel's friend Andy is still in there," Guy replied. "I do not wish to kill his friend. We have to find another means of disposing of the slime. Besides, from what I saw at the restaurant, I believe that the heat ray would no longer have an effect. The slime has joined together in one mass. I am sure that it has become quite large by this point and while the heat ray would damage the creature, I doubt it would kill it completely."

"What about the slime's design?" Squirrel asked. "You told me that it had a shut off switch, right? How do we flip that?"

"It was designed to turn off after consuming a predetermined amount of organic material," Guy answered. "But the amount of material it can consume now has grown exponentially. As I had told you, the impact of bovine growth hormones has yielded unexpected results. It would seem that both the slime's abilities and appetite have grown due to the hormones. The slime is most likely capable of consuming astronomical amounts of organic matter."

"Does the type of material matter?" Travis asked. "I know it was designed to eat garbage, but now that it's eating people shouldn't that turn it off sooner."

"Maybe," Guy shrugged. "But your people have filled their systems with so many non-organic hormones and chemicals that I doubt there would be much of a difference between what is in our landfills and in your digestive systems."

"What if it ate something pure?" Squirrel asked.

"That might work," Guy nodded. "It could overload its system, but it seems unlikely that the slime would consume such a material. It appears to have created a symbiotic relationship with your friend Andy, which most likely means that Andy's emotions, thoughts and appetite are now influencing the slime."

"His thoughts?" Squirrel repeated. He thought about the implications of what Guy had just theorized. Andy was his friend, but Andy was angry. Squirrel had seen it many times before. The only time Andy really seemed happy was when they were lost in a digital world, he was eating fast food or day dreaming about Cece.

An ear-piercing scream echoed through the warehouse.

"Cece!" Squirrel shouted as he dashed from the room.

"Get the girl!" Travis yelled. "Guy, come on, we've got to get your ship working!"

-33-

The world had gone completely insane. In truth, Cece had known it was insane ever since she was twelve and her mother married for the fourth time to a real winner named Allen. He was the kind of guy that Cece immediately knew she should avoid. Whether it was the greasy comb over, the strange oniony odor or the his tendency to end every conversation with a hug, Cece made sure to never be alone in the house with Allen. This fear of step daddy number three is what led Cece to take the job slinging fries at the fast food joint, which was where she got to know Andy.

Cece had passed Andy in the halls of their school, but never stopped to talk to him. Everyone always thought that Cece never had a boyfriend because she thought she was better than everyone or secretly dating an older guy or maybe a lesbian, but the truth was that she was determined to avoid the pitfalls and mistakes of her mother.

However, after graduation Cece had weakened in her resolve and strangely enough found herself crushing on Andy. Maybe it was because he was the polar opposite of every other boy in town or maybe it was because he was kind and gentle? Whatever the reason, Cece found herself taking later shifts so she could have run-ins with Andy. But he was always so painfully shy and never seemed to have the nerve to ask her out.

Cece had grown tired of waiting and finally made up her mind that she was going to ask Andy on a date – convention be damned. Sadly, that was also the night that the world went to hell inside of the restaurant.

"Andy," Cece sniffled as she stood under the warm cascading waters spilling from the showerhead. She wanted to take a shower to wash away the grime and goo from escaping the restaurant, but more than that, she wanted to cry and didn't want the others to see.

What had Andy become? How had he become so angry? He seemed to be losing everything that made him special. That nasty freaking slime was eroding everything that Cece had secretly loved about Andy. Now it seemed like it was too late.

"What happened to you?" Cece choked as she closed her eyes and rested her head against the cheap plastic walls. The water felt good on the back of her neck. It was the only thing that felt good anymore.

Cece's brain swirled with remorse and blame. What if she had asked Andy out sooner? Could this have been avoided or would it have happened anyway?

The shower stall shook, the drainpipe rattling loudly.

"Tax dollars hard at work," Cece gripped. The water was beginning to pool at her feet. "Go down, damn it!" Cece shouted at the water. She moved her foot over the drain and pumped it up and down, trying to create suction to drain the basin.

A thin pink tendril twisted up through the small holes in the drain. It tickled Cece's foot momentarily, causing her to leap back.

"What is that? Hair or something?" Cece wondered out loud.

The metal drain cover burst and hit the ceiling before clattering to the tile floor. Cece screamed and leapt out of the shower as more pink goo pushed through the drainpipe and into the shower basin.

"Cece!" Squirrel yelled as he burst through the door and into the bathroom. He stumbled as he encountered a naked and soaking wet Cece.

"Come on, perv!" Cece shouted, rushing past the wide-eyed boy. "We need to get the hell out of here!"

"Not looking! Not looking!" Squirrel shouted as he threw a towel to Cece. She wrapped the towel around her body and grabbed the black jumpsuit Travis had given her to change into. Squirrel snatched her shoes from the corner.

Pink slime spewed from the broken drainpipe. Jets of the foul material shot upwards, spattering the ceiling and stretching across towards Cece and Squirrel. Tentacles stretched from each pool, lashing at the two as they fled.

Even though they were the only two in the room, Cece and Squirrel heard a third voice.

"Ceceeeeee! Ceceeeeeeeeeeeee!" a garbled voice rattled out of the drain.

"Holy shit, it's Andy!" Squirrel yelled as they ran from the bathroom.

"Who the hell did you think it would be?" Cece panted.

"Run for the main room," Squirrel replied, ignoring Cece's sarcasm. "Guy and Travis are waiting at the ship!"

Cece sprinted past the dingy windows of the warehouse. Shadows moved outside. She hoped it was the soldiers going after Andy.

One of the shadows burst through the window falling on Cece. It was another of the pink slime monsters. It's skeletal face smiled with wicked glee as it pawed at the girl, somehow causing her no harm.

Squirrel grabbed a nearby fire extinguisher and sprayed the creature, but three more spilled through the shattered window. Cece struggled beneath the creatures, but the slime kept her pinned. The skeletons swam through the sea of pink ooze and organs, passing from one mass to the next until their pointed fingers found purchase in Cece's hair.

The writhing ball of slime leapt up from the floor and dove back through the window. Cece was gone.

"Let's go, kid! There's nothing more we can do here!" Travis shouted as he grabbed Squirrel's arm and pulled him towards Guy's ship. "We got the ship working, but those things are everywhere. They've taken out my entire team. There are just too many!"

Squirrel and Travis sprinted up the ramp into Guy's ship. It was already lifting off the ground as the ramp slid shut.

"Please hold on to something!" Guy cried as he pushed the controls forward and the ship burst through the corrugated metal roof of the old warehouse. The ship shuddered from the impact but continued upwards.

Once at a safe height, Guy stopped the ship, hovering above the warehouse. He switched on a screen and the three occupants watched massive pink tentacles close around the warehouse like the fingers on a giant's hand. The warehouse disappeared in the deafening chorus of screeching metal and crunching glass.

"What do we do now?" Squirrel asked. "He took Cece. He took your entire team. It's only us. We can't stop him by ourselves. It's huge. Andy won."

-34-

The slime coursed deeper into Andy's body. He had let it in, but could never have known how much. The slime broke apart into single cell organisms and implanted itself in the large fatty deposits of Andy's body. The fat, rife with bovine growth hormones, fed the organisms, fueling their replication and growth. Single cell organisms swelled and grew, bulging from Andy's body at sickening angles.

Andy screamed within the center of the giant slime mold, but the pink tentacles kept him firmly rooted to his morbid throne.

Relax, Andy. Stop fighting.

"Please stop! Please stop!" Andy screamed, his words coming out as a series of pink, frothy bubbles that burst and vanished in the writhing pile of goo.

Pockets of grotesquely bulged skin undulated and pulsed, growing more fervent with each agonizing second. Something new and terrible trembled beneath Andy's skin, hungry and eager to be released.

Andy tried to fight his own body, but knew that he had no control. The slime would do as it pleased.

Just relax, Andy. New friends are coming to play. Don't you want more help punishing those that hurt you? Just relax. Let them out. This is what you wanted, Andy.

"Nooooo!" Andy screamed, but it was too late. Small black talons pierced his skin, cutting from inside his own body. The claws wiggled, as if the creatures were slowly learning their own abilities and new bodies.

Andy continued to scream, tears streaming down his face, but all was lost in the burbling mass of the pink slime. The wicked claws, tipped with obsidian-like points, continued to cut.

Just relax, Andy. New friends are coming to play. Don't you want more help punishing those that hurt you? Just relax. Let them out. Let them out or Cece will suffer, Andy. We'll absorb her and she'll be gone. Didn't you do this for Cece? It would be terrible to lose her now. Let them out, Andy. LET THEM OUT RIGHT NOW! RIGHT NOW OR CECE DIES! Remember, this is what you wanted, Andy. This is what you wanted...

-35-

"What'd you mean the slime's design is based on insect biology?" Travis snapped. He had been pacing the small confines of Guy's ship for the last half hour. The ship hovered above the town as the three occupants watched Andy and the pink slime lay waste to everything below. Ideas and hope both seemed to be in short supply.

"Ants and bees," Guy answered. "We needed to design the slime cells to work together to break down organic material so my people incorporated traits from insects commonly found on Earth."

"So the slime is what? Like a bug or something?" Squirrel asked. He sat in the strange chair once again, now afraid of things far worse than an anal probing.

"In actions, perhaps," Guy nodded, "but the slime is not actually an insect, at least not in the biological sense."

"Okay," Travis exhaled as he stopped pacing, "so the slime acts like a bug. What's that mean for us? Is it going to build a hive or something?"

"In a sense it already has," Guy clarified. "The slime itself is the hive. It has joined together to be its own mobile hive, but I do not think that the slime will form an actual stationary home. It, rather Andy, knows that would be far too risky."

"Andy knows?" Squirrel repeated. "So Andy is like the queen bee? Ants and bees always have a queen, right? Like one bug that lords over all the others."

"Yes, they do," Guy agreed, "but the social structure employed by those insects is based upon reproductive abilities. It is true that the slime has the ability to reproduce asexually, but it can only make more slime that way. I think it has bigger plans now."

"Reproductive abilities?" Travis sneered. "So your boy Andy is going to get knocked up by the slime? Is that even possible?"

"No," Guy added, "it is not possible. Andy does not have the ability to reproduce in the manner that the slime requires. He was simply a carrier for the organism and now functions as little more than nucleus for the larger slime mold. I do not think Andy is being kept alive for anything beyond an informational resource.

The slime has undoubtedly accessed his memory and is now using that information to its advantage."

"Right," Travis agreed. "So Andy is more of a library than a prom date for the slime, which means that your whole idea of a queen is bunk, right?"

"Not necessarily," Guy shook his massive egg-shaped head. "It means that…"

"It means that Cece is probably still alive," Squirrel cut in, "and in a hell of a lot more trouble than we thought."

-36-

The pain in Andy's body was beyond naming. It defied logic and explanation. It simply was. It was all things, all sensations. It was all he had at the moment. But Andy stopped fighting. He let the pain come and grow, blossom into something terrible and excruciating. He would endure for Cece.

The creatures forced their way out of his body shredding his flesh with black claws. The tattered ribbons of skin knitted back together only to be slashed by another eager set of claws. Through teary eyes, Andy watched as the new monsters, black and shiny, slithered out of his body and wriggled through the pink slime. Each reached the edge and sprang forth in a spewing burst of pink excitement.

The creatures, at least twenty or so, landed on four unsteady legs, trembling before finding their footing. They shook like an army of dogs emerging from a pink slimy lake.

Andy, still in his throne of organs and bone, watched the little monsters stretch and grow, at first no bigger than a small dog, but now incredibly muscular and at least four feet long. A thin tail, like some hellish paintbrush, swished to and fro. Some of the creatures, now free of their slimy coating, revealed coats of either brown and white, or black and white. One, larger than the rest by half, remained completely black as if born from the deepest pits of a coal shaft in the center of Hell. The larger creature turned and glared at Andy with glowing pink eyes. Its expression was one born of equal parts hatred and devotion. Andy felt an involuntary shudder pass through his body.

There is no need to be fearful, Andy. Do not fear what you have created. What WE have created.

"What the hell are they?" Andy screamed.

They are yours. They are your army. They live to protect us, Andy, to keep us safe from those who would seek to cause us harm.

"Like soldiers?" Andy asked.

The creatures all turned to face Andy, lining up behind the larger black one. Their faces were a demonic interpretation of cows. Long twisted black horns jutted from either side of their broad, flat heads. Large muscular legs that ended in three black claws flexed as the monsters obediently sat down before Andy.

Yes, Andy. They are soldiers, designed to protect the hive.

"The hive?" Andy questioned. "What hive?" *This hive. Andy, we ARE the hive. All that remains is to crown our queen. Then, only then, will our plans come to fruition. We need a queen. YOU need a queen!*

"Cece," Andy whispered, answering his own question. "Where is she?"

She is here, Andy. She is safe...for now. She will remain safe if you can convince her to become our queen. Otherwise, she will share the same fate as the others, as those who hurt you.

"Bring her to me," Andy demanded. "I want to see her now!"

Of course.

The soldiers stepped aside as Cece walked through their herd. One walked behind her snapping at the back of her legs with a wicked mouthful of crooked black fangs. Long strings of pink drool hung from its mouth and it flecked Cece's skin with each vicious snap.

"Andy!" Cece cried. Her voice trembled. "Andy please! Please don't hurt me!"

"Hurt you?" Andy laughed. He closed his eyes and willed his throne to move closer to the edge of the slime mold. "Cece, I would never hurt you. I am here to save you. I am here to make you a queen, my queen."

"What are you talking about, Andy?" Cece quivered. Tears streamed down her cheeks, but the soldier nudged her forward.

Andy concentrated, willing the slime to do his bidding. Small pink tentacles dashed about assembling a throne of similar design to Andy's own.

"This is yours," Andy motioned to the revolting chair. "You will rule from here as my queen. You can have anything, Cece, anything at all. You just have to say yes. Say that you'll be my queen."

"Your queen?" Cece sneered. "Andy, look around. Why the hell would I want to be the queen of this? You've killed half the town."

"I killed them for you!" Andy screamed. "These people are nothing more than food. They looked down on us, made fun of us and now, now we will rule over them! No one will ever laugh at us again!"

"Rule over them? There's no one left! Andy, I never wanted any of this," Cece said softly. "I'm sorry, Andy, but my answer is no. Do whatever you're going to do, but I'm not going to be your queen. There was a time when I would have wanted that, but now, I don't even want to be your friend. Just kill me or eat me or whatever gross thing you have planned and get it over with." Cece took a deep breath, exhaled slowly and turned her back on Andy.

The second throne disassembled and vanished into the slime as Andy roared with rage.

Cece opened her eyes to see one of the demonic cow creatures spring forward, its mouth gaping and filled with a nest of hellish teeth. This was how it would end, but at least it was on her terms. Cece would play no role in Andy's sick world, even if that meant death by demonic cow.

-37-

The metal panel in front of Squirrel rippled and took on the appearance of mercury. A thin tendril stretched from the center and reached for the side of the boy's head.

"You sure about this?" Squirrel said hesitantly as he moved his head away from the silver thread.

"The weapons system on my ship work through a neural interface," Guy explained. "My attention must be devoted to operating the flight system. Typically, there would be at least three operators for a ship of this size."

"At least it's not an anal interface," Travis smirked.

"Ha-ha-ha," Squirrel replied. "Why don't you do this? You're the trained government killer."

"My computer determined that you are a more suitable candidate," Guy said. "Your brain is programmed to accept the demands of the weapons targeting system due to your repetitive playing of video games."

"Alright," Squirrel sighed, "just get it over with."

The thin strand of quicksilver reached for Squirrel. As it did, the end frayed and split into hundreds of microscopic filaments. The filaments brushed Squirrel's temple before passing through the pores of his skin and traveling to his brain.

"Kind of itches," Squirrel said. "Like tiny bugs or something."

"Please do not scratch at it," Guy said over his shoulder. His attention was now turned to a set of controls that emerged from a wall near his seat.

"Um, okay," Squirrel grunted as his fingers dropped back to the armrest of his chair. "But when do I know if this worked."

"Close your eyes and reopen them slowly," Guy said. "The interface should be complete at that point."

Squirrel closed his eyes and when he reopened them, a small image appeared in the corner of his eye. It something akin to the picture-in-picture feature on TVs, but it was seamless and streamed images from outside the ship.

"I see the slime...and something else," Squirrel leaned forward and the image zoomed in. "They look like cows on steroids, but worse."

"The slime must be creating warriors to protect the hive," Guy added.

"The slimy skeletal monsters weren't doing a good enough job?" Travis barked.

"Those were scavengers," Guy answered. "They're purpose was to gather more food for the slime."

"You mean people," Squirrel said flatly.

"Yes, people," Guy paused, "regrettably. These new creations must have been made with the sole purpose of protecting the main organism. It makes sense that the slime would draw upon bovine DNA for reference while creating a new life form being that those building blocks were readily available."

"Crap!" Squirrel shouted. "Cece is down there in the middle of those things and I can see Andy on the edge of the slime. How do I make the weapons…NO!" Squirrel watched in horror as one of the creatures leapt towards Cece, its mouth open and fangs bared.

The ship rocked back as a massive burst of energy released from one of its cannons. Squirrel's eyes momentarily flashed a brilliant ruby red as he watched the beam disintegrate the monster attacking Cece. Ashes rained down around Cece.

"Shoot Andy!" Travis yelled. "Shoot him now while he's exposed!"

Squirrel hesitated. Could he really turn his best friend into a smoldering pile of ashes? Was that thing even his friend?

"SHOOT HIM!" Travis bellowed as he shook Squirrel's shoulders.

"I do not see another alternative," Guy said sadly. "I am sorry, Squirrel."

Squirrel squeezed his eyes shut and envisioned the attack. The microscopic metal runners sent the message from his brain to the ship's computer, but it was too late. Andy had already pulled back into the main heap of slime. Had Squirrel not hesitated, he would have hit Andy, but as it was, all he accomplished was sizzling a large section of the slime.

Thick clouds of steamy smoke filled the air. The slime was already oozing back into the space emptied by the blast from the ship's cannon. Andy was little more than a blurry shadow at the slime's center.

"Damn it!" Travis screamed. "Why'd you hesitate? We had him! Damn it Squirrel! Damn it!"

"Is this what is commonly known as a temper tantrum?" Guy asked.

"Shut up!" Travis sulked.

"I took the shot," Squirrel protested. "I missed. What do you want me to do? Cece is down there and Andy is – was my friend. You want to trade places, secret agent man? Because I'd love to stop shooting at my friends!"

"Sorry," Travis muttered. "You tried. I know."

"Incoming!" Guy's voice chirped. The ship's monitors showed a large pick up truck spiraling through the air towards the ship. "Please hold onto something!"

The ship pitched to the right and dropped ten feet in the air, but the truck's cab clipped the side of the ship.

Alarms and flashing lights filled the ship as Guy struggled to regain control of the ship.

"It's not responding properly," Guy explained.

Squirrel struggled to stay focused on the slime, Andy and Cece. He would need to make sure his next shot counted, but the world refused to stop spinning.

Three more cars were pitched towards the ship. Squirrel fired wild shots.

"Why won't it do what it's supposed to?" Travis barked. He wanted to do something and found doing nothing almost unbearable. "Your ships move at unnatural angles all the time."

"You tell me!" Guy shouted back. "Your people were the ones investigating my ship. There's no telling what they did."

"I thought they couldn't get in," Travis snarled. "I thought you had this all figured out! Don't you know how to fly this thing?"

"I may have lost my concentration when the slime began attacking your secure warehouse," Guy snapped acerbically. Squirrel was shocked to see the alien acting petulantly. "I do not know!"

"Focus, damn it!" Squirrel bellowed as another car crashed against the side of the ship.

Guy pushed the controls forward and the ship shot upward. Moments later, a visible ripple passed through the ship's interior and it jolted to a sudden stop.

"There is a problem," Guy's four thin fingers knotted in a tight fist and repeatedly smashed a series of buttons. "The slime has grabbed the ship."

Squirrel's eyes rolled in his sockets as he tried to get a visual on the slime. He could only see pink. "I don't have a shot!"

"It is covering the entire ship," Guy replied. "Travis, you need to get into the seat with Squirrel."

"What?" Travis asked.

"Just sit on my lap!" Squirrel yelled. The ship rocked back and forth. Travis stumbled forward, grabbed the side of the chair to steady himself and then climbed into Squirrel's lap. "And what would you like for Christmas?" Squirrel grunted.

"A new job," Travis snapped.

Guy clambered onto Travis's lap. "Squirrel concentrate on jettisoning the chair from the ship. See it in your mind and force the image out. You must concentrate."

A deafening metallic screech filled the interior of the small ship. Pink slime began to spill through the cracks.

"Any time you're ready, Squirrel!" Travis shouted. A tendril of pink slime shot forward towards the agent's face. Travis dodged the slime, but left an opening for it to hit the side of Squirrel's face.

Squirrel screamed in agony as the skin on the right side of his face sizzled, falling away in wet chunks. The pain was intense, worse than anything Squirrel had ever felt, even worse than the time his butane lighter exploded in his pants and set his underwear on fire. Still, Squirrel concentrated. He needed to envision an escape pod.

The floor beneath the chair trembled. Ripples danced across the floor.

"Keep going!" Travis yelled.

More slime oozed into the ship's interior.

The silvery metal turned liquid and climbed the sides of the chair. Travis squeezed his eyes shut. Squirrel continued to focus. Guy never moved.

A large pink tentacle tipped with a wicked hook peeled the side of Guy's ship like a cheap aluminum can. The metal melted beneath the slime's touch.

As the ship fell away in shimmering quicksilver raindrops a large almond shaped object twisted upward like a drunken bottle rocket before vanishing in the night sky.

-38-

She said no, Andy. She denied your offer, OUR offer, to be queen. She is not worthy, does not deserve the honor you offered. She is no different than the others.

"Shut up!" Andy snapped. "She just needs time! Stop trying to make me hurt her. I won't hurt Cece!"

You may refuse, but our soldiers will not. She is food and will be treated as such!

A wave of pink slime shot forward and formed a quivering wall between Cece and the slavering soldiers.

"You think you're the only one who's learned things?" Andy grinned. "You became part of me, but I'm part of you as well! I won't, no WE won't hurt Cece!"

As you wish, Andy.

The soldiers turned away from where they clawed at the rubbery wall separating them from Cece. The larger black one swiped one more time, howled and then went to sit amongst the others.

"She needs time to understand," Andy said. "Threats aren't going to work. I need time to make Cece see why she wants to be queen. You can't just threaten to kill her and expect her to do what you want."

So it would seem. With the alien craft destroyed, it is safe for you to be exposed again. If she presents any threat to you, Andy, the soldiers will kill her. You understand that, correct?

"Yes," Andy growled. "Now move Cece over to the roof of that building and then me. I want time alone with her."

You are never alone, Andy.

"I do not want to be disturbed!" Andy bellowed. "It is the only way to convince her!" His anger sent trembling waves dancing across the amorphous pink blob.

As you wish, Andy.

The pink wall slipped beneath Cece's feet and lifted her off the ground. It moved high above the soldiers. Most appeared indifferent, but Andy noticed that the black one, the one he decided to name Midnight, stared intently, its eyes fixed upon

Cece and its toothy maw chewing the empty space between its jaws.

Andy was lowered onto the roof still seated in his throne. The collection of bones clinked lightly as they scraped on the thick tarpaper roof.

"Make a table!" Andy commanded. "And bring back Cece's chair!"

A thick arm of pink slime settled between Cece and Andy. He smiled with satisfaction as he watched bones and organs trickle down through the slime forming an ornate table. A throne, matching Andy's exactly, was placed on the empty side of the table.

Cece looked scared, but Andy figured that was to be expected.

"Please sit," Andy smiled. "Nothing is going to happen to you."

A loud noise, something akin to fingernails raking across a chalkboard, rattled through the night air. As three soldiers clambered over the edge of the building, Andy realized the sound was their obsidian-like claws digging into the bricks on the side of the building.

"They're here to protect us," Andy nodded towards the creatures. "I know they look scary, but don't worry, Cece. I promise, I won't let anything happen to you. I just want to talk."

Cece's mouth hung open and then snapped shut. She took a deep breath, exhaled slowly and carefully lowered herself into the revolting chair.

"Thank you," Andy grinned. "I'll admit that this was not how I saw our first date going, but what are you gonna do, right? I mean things have obviously changed."

"Date?" Cece muttered. A thick rope of intestine tangled itself around her ankle. She cried out in shock and shook it from her leg.

Andy tried to keep his laughter inside and failed miserably.

"Oh man," Andy chortled. "The look on your face is priceless, totally priceless!"

"So glad I could provide a little comic relief for you, Andy," Cece snapped. The soldiers growled and stalked forward, but Andy waved them away.

"Cece," Andy sighed, "I'm going to be blunt because time is not really on our side here. Besides, I wasted plenty of time not being direct with you and look where that got us?"

"This has nothing to do with me!" Cece growled. "I'm not responsible for any of this!"

Andy grinned and settled back into his throne. "I'm sure that you need to tell yourself that right now, but once you're part of this, you'll see it differently."

"I already told you that I'm not going to be your freaking queen!" Cece shouted. "I'm not going to do anything that you want, Andy. You're sick! You're a sick, disgusting monster!"

"I'm sick?" Andy repeated, feigning a look of offense. "No, Cece I am not the sick one. This world and the people in it, those are the ones who are sick, not me. I am the result of their sickness. If the world were kind, if it were fair, then we wouldn't be here right now, would we? I am simply the effect of all the violence, the prejudice and cruelty that is forced on people like you and me. If the world treated us right, then I never would have become this!"

"You still had a choice, Andy," Cece sniffled. "You still could have tried to have been better. That's what I liked about you or at least I used to."

"You liked me?" Andy asked, a look of true shock on his face.

"I did," Cece nodded. "Now, I'm not even sure what you are, let alone if I like you."

Reddened anger flushed over Andy's face. "See! See! That right there! That is what I'm talking about!"

A wave of pink slime crushed a nearby building. Burbled cries leaked from the wreckage. One man tried to run, but Midnight was on him in a matter of seconds. Flesh and bone flew wildly as Midnight tore into the man. A few other soldiers loped towards the kill, but the larger black one snapped at them and snarled until they backed away. Midnight tore one more long stringy bit of wet muscle from the man's back with a sickening snap. He loped off to the side, chewing the wad of meat and sat down to watch the other soldiers fight over his scraps.

"That is what you were talking about?" Cece thrust her finger towards the monsters snarling over the tangled remains of the man. "That is your vision of fair and kind, Andy?"

"No," Andy agreed, "but what choice did they leave me? I never asked for any of this. I never asked for a father that would leave my mom for a tiny deformed stripper or a mother that would hang herself with a pair of my underwear! I never asked for any of that, but there's my life, Cece. And look at yours! Did you ask for anything that life gave or took from you? Huh? I didn't think so, Cece! But there you have it. Assholes like that guy get whatever they want and people like you and me get the shit end of the stick for no reason at all!" Andy's shoulders heaved.

"Ask for it?" Cece laughed. "Jeez, Andy you didn't even know that guy. How can you pass judgment on him? Who knows? Maybe his life had twice as many midget strippers and underwear related suicides? Maybe his life was even worse than yours? But you wouldn't know that, because you sent your disgusting cow monsters to eat him."

"No one's life is worse than mine!" Andy pouted.

"Really?" Cece sneered. "Really now? You sound like a spoiled little shit, Andy! No one has a life that's worse than yours? Everyone's life sucks, Andy! That's just life. Grow a set and deal with it. Everyone says crap like it's not fair, no one has it as bad as me and that's why things never get better. You spend all your time blaming everyone else. It's always someone else's fault. It has nothing to do with the fact that you're being a whiny bitch and doing nothing, not one damn thing, to make your life any better!"

Andy laughed deeply. "That's where you're wrong, Cece. For the first time in my life, I'm working to make things better. I'm going to make the entire world better. No one will be better than anyone else! No one will be pretty or ugly or fat or skinny. They will all be part of one whole, part of me!"

"So you get to decide?" Cece demanded. "You're the measure of what the world should be? Who gave you that role, Andy?"

"They did!" Andy sent another slime wave through the side of a nearby church. Parishioners, trying to find sanctuary, were lost beneath the roiling pink ooze. "They made me into this! They decided!"

"You still had a choice!" Cece stamped her foot. A wet coil of intestine squished beneath her foot and she immediately regretted her action. "You always have a choice!"

"And so do you," Andy smiled, but his expression held no humor or mirth. "And now you have to decide, Cece. I'd think real hard if I were you and carefully pick the next words out of your mouth."

-39-

The interior of the escape pod was beyond cramped. Two humans and an alien did not leave much space for anything beyond breathing. Guy tried to turn his bulbous head to look at Squirrel. The boy had been injured by the slime, Guy had seen that much, yet he was still concentrating on holding their small craft together.

"How you doing, kid?" Travis asked. He still sat on Squirrel's lap, but then again, there was nowhere else to sit. He shifted the small alien on his lap. Guy was light, but the tiny scales covering his body plucked and pulled at Travis' suit. One or two of the tiny iridescent scales poked through and dug into his thigh.

"I'm fine," Squirrel forced the words between his teeth. "Just let me focus on what I'm doing, okay?"

"He is right, agent Travis," Guy chimed in. "Should Squirrel lose his concentration, the entire craft could disassemble. That would be most unfortunate, indeed."

"Indeed," Travis sneered.

The escape pod rocketed across the night sky. Squirrel had no idea where he was going. He just wanted to get away from Andy, from town, from the slime. What was left for him to do other than run? He tried to stop Andy, tried to save Cece, but he had failed miserably. There was nothing left to do but run. But even as Squirrel willed the ship to move faster, some part of him knew that running was at best, a temporary solution.

Andy wasn't slowing down. He was larger and meaner with every passing second. Most of the town had been destroyed or eaten. The police never even had a chance to call in the army. Sure, Travis and his people had shown up, but Andy had eaten most of them and it would be a long time before any one else from the agency came to check on them. Travis and his people worked in secret, complete black ops, so an extended period of communication blackouts wouldn't be unheard of. By the time anyone realized what Andy and the slime were doing, it would be too late – it looked like it already was.

The escape pod rocked back and forth as if being gently tossed by waves. Squirrel squeezed his eyes shut and willed the craft to move forward, but it felt frozen in place.

"We're not moving," Squirrel said, his voice cracking with stress. "I'm trying to move, but we can't. Do you think Andy has grabbed us? Could he really have reached this high?"

"I don't think so," Travis said. "If it was Andy, he would be peeling us like an onion." Travis couldn't help but look at the acidic burns on the side of the young boy's face. An uncomfortable mix of admiration and sadness swirled through Travis. He had seen lesser wounds cripple grown men, men who had been trained to be tough and ignore pain, yet this little hippie was taking it all in stride. He didn't look it, but Squirrel had to be one tough son of a bitch.

"I agree," Guy reached out to touch the walls of the escape pod. Intense vibrations danced through his slender fingers. It felt like the pod had suddenly found itself in the middle of a massive beehive. "It would appear that we have problems that extend beyond Andy and the slime."

"What else is new?" Travis groaned.

-40-

Cece watched as Andy sent out waves of slime and droves of cow monsters to devour what was left of their hometown. People she had grown up with, some she liked and some she didn't, vanished in an moments of intense pain, but regardless of who they were, Cece felt her heart break with each death.

"Andy!" Cece shouted. "Andy, stop and I'll do it!"

The slime shuddered to a stop and Andy emerged, once again seated in his throne.

"You'll be my queen?" Andy smiled. His eyes rolled back and he nodded. "I mean our queen."

"I'll do whatever you want," Cece whimpered. "I don't even care anymore. Just stop hurting people." Cece knew that Andy could lie; that the slime most likely would, but she figured there was no other choice. She had to do something, even if it was something completely revolting.

"I knew you'd make the right choice. You always were so smart, Cece, and beautiful too," Andy cooed. The second throne reassembled from the devoured bits of victims and emerged next to Andy. A sticky arm of pink goo thrust it towards Cece.

The coils of intestine pulled at Cece's clothes as jagged edges of bone poked at her back and legs. She closed her eyes and held her breath as the slime closed around her.

-41-

The escape pod was silently pulled into the massive triangular ship that hovered motionlessly above town. A series of colored lights danced across the outside of the gigantic ship. Travis and Squirrel had no idea what was happening. Guy appeared in the know, but remained reticent.

A shudder passed over the pod. Light steps padded around the outside.

"Relax your mind, Squirrel," Guy sighed. "There is no point resisting."

Squirrel took in a deep breath and exhaled slowly. The walls of the escape pod shimmered, a ripple spreading from the middle before they melted away in waves of quicksilver.

A large group of intensely angry looking aliens surrounded the occupants of the pod. Guy grunted and jumped down from Travis' lap. His feet padded silently through the shimmering puddle.

"What's going on?" Squirrel whispered.

"No freaking idea," Travis muttered.

A series of high pitched squeaks and pops passed between Guy and a larger alien of similar appearance. Squirrel leaned forward.

"Get off me," he grunted as he pushed out of the chair. Somehow, maybe because of the neural implant, Squirrel could make out some of the words flying between the two aliens. "I think that's his..."

"This is my mother," Guy sighed as the other alien slapped him on the back of the head.

"Your mother?" Travis asked. "Seriously?"

"Oh, he is very serious," Guy's mother replied, her slender arms bowing out as she placed her hands on her hips. "And so is the amount of trouble that he is in. I cannot believe you. Your father and I were worried sick. And what will the neighbors think? But do you care? Ohhh, nooo. Of course not. Why would you care that everyone thinks our son is thief and liar?"

"Mother, please," Guy pleaded. He turned to face his friends. "I was not completely honest with you and for that. I apologize."

"That is a start," his mother snapped.

"The ship I arrived in was not my own," Guy confessed. "It was my father's and I did not tell him I was taking it."

"He completely went insane!" Guy's mother chided. "That was his birthday present to himself and you brought it to Earth of all places and destroyed it. Why? Why would you do this?"

"I could not let the humans suffer because of our mistake," Guy argued. "It is wrong!"

"There you go with your right and wrong again," she snorted. "So full of ideas. I was like that too when I was young, but you can't steal your father's ship to carry out your liberal agenda."

"Whoa, whoa," Travis held his hands up. "Are you telling me you're just some punk teenager who stole his daddy's midlife crisis to go do some hippy shit? And now your mommy and her friends came to pick you up in their intergalactic minivan? My god, we are so screwed! So freaking screwed!"

"Do not disparage my son like that," Guy's mother waved a thin finger at Travis.

"Mother," Guy began.

"Do not 'Mother' me, young man," she snapped. "You are done playing with your friends for the day. It is time to go home."

"Go home?" Squirrel yelled. "Lady, are you nuts? We need Guy to help us. The slime your people made is destroying my town!"

"Humans are so disrespectful," Guy's mother shook her head to the other aliens. "He is grounded and you will just have to clean up your own mess. We will drop you off somewhere safe."

"Safe?" Travis snorted. "Haven't you seen what's going on down there?"

"There is a building the slime has not destroyed," Guy's mother replied. "We will place you there."

"What building?" Guy demanded. "Mother, what building?"

"There," she pointed to a large screen. A single building stood in the midst of a writhing pink sea. Small hellish cow monsters leapt between the frothing rose-colored waves.

"Holy crap! That's my parent's health food store," Squirrel added.

"Then it is the perfect place to leave you," Guy's mother cut in. She turned and prepared to send Travis and Squirrel back down to Earth.

Guy rushed forward and grabbed Squirrel's elbow. "Concentrate," he insisted. "You still have the neural link. Draw the remains of the pod into your body. You will need the material. Make it into anything you can imagine."

Squirrel had so many questions, but knew time was limited. He closed his eyes and drew the silvery material into his body. He could feel it sloshing through his veins.

"Why is that building left standing?" Travis shouted as a bright beam of blue light appeared around him and Squirrel.

"Organic material!" Guy yelled back.

"Organic material?" Travis asked, but he was already on the roof of the health food store. Squirrel appeared seconds later.

"What do we do now?" Travis yelled as he eyed three heavily muscled nightmares. The creatures rode the next surge of pink slime onto the roof. Jaws yawned open, revealing crooked nests of black fangs that dripped thick strings of pink saliva.

"We fight," Squirrel growled as he closed his eyes and concentrated.

-42-

Andy's happiness at finally having Cece for his own vanished in a flash of blue light. Squirrel and some man in a wrinkled, but expensive looking suit, appeared on the roof of the health food store.

"SQUIRRELLLLLL!!!" Andy bellowed as both he and the slime surged forward. Squirrel had tried to take Cece from him before and Andy wasn't going to allow that. Squirrel probably wanted Cece for himself.

Andy called to the soldiers, called to Midnight directly, and sent them galloping towards his former friend. Squirrel and whoever this other man was, would be Andy's wedding night feast.

-43-

Travis pulled his gun and emptied an entire magazine into the forehead of the nearest monster. It grunted and bled thick pink blood, but didn't stop and sure as hell didn't die.

"We're screwed," Travis yelled as he slapped another magazine into the gun. He began firing again as the nearest creature leapt for his neck.

A glistening metallic spike raced past Travis's head, spearing the monster through its large bovine eyes. Travis could see the end of the spike jutting out from the other side of the creature's head. It twitched a few times, as if trying to run in the air. The spike withdrew and the creature fell motionless to the roof.

"Get behind me," Squirrel commanded.

The next two monsters launched themselves at the same time. Squirrel closed his eyes and held his arms out towards them. The creatures' mouths closed around his arms. Travis was sure Squirrel was going to die. A collection of jagged metallic quills burst from all sides of the creatures' boxy heads.

Squirrel pulled his arms free from the dead monsters' mouths. It was then that Travis saw the burns on Squirrel's face had vanished and the new wounds on his arms were rapidly knitting themselves back together.

"How are you doing that?" Travis gasped.

Squirrel shrugged. "Guy told me to concentrate on taking the rest of the escape pod into my body. Once he knew that I could use the neural link, I think he wanted to give us a weapon so we'd stand a chance."

"Then why was he yelling at me about organic matter before I got beamed down here?" Travis barked.

Squirrel thought for a moment. "That's why the slime hasn't touched this place. Once it consumes enough organic matter, it shuts down. It has been eating people that are filled with toxic crap from what they eat. That's how it's been able to keep growing bigger and bigger. Andy knows my parents' store is full of health food and is probably worried that wrecking this place would max out the slime and shut it down."

"Okay," Travis nodded. "Still, I don't see how that helps. I don't think Andy is really in the mood for wheat grass right now."

A burst of red light erupted from Squirrel's eyes. Three nearby cow monsters crumbled into piles of smoldering ash. "Ow, that kind of stung." Squirrel rubbed his eyes with the back of his hand.

Squirrel turned and kicked open one of the nearby skylights. "Go inside and grab some food. I don't think it matters what, but grab as much as you can carry. I think I know how to stop Andy, but I need to test something out."

"You going to be okay up here alone?" Travis asked.

Squirrel spun in a tight circle, his hands sharpened like blades. Bits of cow monster rained down around him.

"I think I'll manage," Squirrel smirked.

The inside of the health food store was oddly silent. Travis tired to ignore the disconcerting silence, but it pressed in upon him.

"Get back, looter!" a skinny man with bad dreadlocks and sandals yelled. He held a can of soy protein high over his head. "We can all share, man, but you can't steal. That's just not cool, man, not cool!"

"Drop the soy," Travis grunted as he grabbed a sack of quinoa from the shelf. The large can of soy powder collided with the side of Travis' head. "Damn it! That hurt!" Travis had to fight the urge to draw his gun. "I'm not stealing. Squirrel is on the roof. He needs this!"

"Squirrel?" the old hippy asked. "Man, you're friends with my little dude? I'm super sorry about hitting you with that soy powder, man. It's just that things are like totally whack-a-do outside. Some crazy government experiment gone wrong or something, I bet."

"You have no idea. Help me get as much of this crap to roof as possible," Travis barked. He and the old hippy began loading bag after bag of grain, flour and powders onto the roof.

"Hey, Squirrel," the hippy called. "How goes it, little dude?"
"Dad, get back inside!" Squirrel yelled as he lanced a cow monster with one hand and decapitated it with the other.

"Oh no," his dad moaned. "No way, man. My boy is up here killing animals? No way. I taught you better than that, Squirrel!"

"Get him inside!" Squirrel yelled.

"Sir, I'd suggest you listen to your son," Travis said as he pushed the hippy back through the window. "Those aren't animals. They are a combination of government screw up and alien technology."

"Oh, well why didn't you say so," he nodded as the closed the skylight.

"Throw some of the food off the edge of the building," Squirrel yelled as he fought with a cow monster. The slime surged around the building, but wouldn't actually come into contact with it.

Travis hurled a bag of wheatgrass powder off the roof of the health food store. He fired a shot, ripping it open and raining grainy green powder all over the nearby slime. A loud sizzle and pop filled the night air. Somewhere in the distance, a scream rumbled.

"It hurt it!" Travis reported. "The slime turned black and crumbled!"

"Then why aren't you throwing more?" Squirrel screamed.

Travis threw more and more organic food from the roof, as Squirrel cut down any cow monsters unlucky enough to come close. The slime ingested the organic material and shut down, but more rolled in to the take its place.

"We're running out of food," Travis yelled as he hurled a bag of quinoa into the air.

"This was only a test," Squirrel growled.

-44-

The soldiers were dying. Squirrel was killing them with some sort of alien technology that brought to mind the evil Terminator in the second movie. Andy couldn't help but be a little impressed – a little impressed and a whole lot pissed. Andy moved his soldiers into small groups and gave them each precise orders, just like he did with digital ones in video games. But just like the last time he had faced Squirrel in battle, his friend was making short work of Andy's troops.

"Midnight!" Andy bellowed. The creature finished snapping the arm off a townie and turned to face him. "Get them! I let you hang back, but now I need you."

Midnight faltered, as if unwilling to follow Andy's orders.

NOW! The command vibrated through the massive pile of slime and the monster bounded towards the roof of the health food store.

Andy watched with a sense of satisfaction as the alpha of his soldiers leapt onto the roof. It cornered the man in the suit. The suit fired wildly, but the bullets had little effect. Andy felt pride as the monster's massive jaws closed around the man's arm. He wanted to be closer. He longed to feel the skulls of his enemies splinter beneath his feet, but the slime refused to allow him to get near the store.

Patience, Andy. Patience.

"You saw what they did," Andy protested. "They know how to hurt us!"

They know nothing, Andy! All they have accomplished is disabling an inconsequential amount of slime. We wait and they die. Patience, Andy. They do not have anything strong enough to stop us. Patience.

-45-

A hulking black monster crashed down onto the roof. Travis spun and began firing, more out of reflex than anything. Bullets weren't working, but what else could he do? A swift kick sent a bag of unbleached whole-wheat flour smashing into the monster's face. A brownish white cloud exploded, but did little more than coat the creature's inky hide with contrasting tan dots.

"Squirrel! The hippy food doesn't work on the cow monsters!" Travis screamed as he fired at the creature's large glassy eyes hoping to find a weak spot.

"Didn't think it would," Squirrel grunted as he decapitated another monster, his back turned to the agent.

Travis howled in pain as the monster's tangled mess of fangs closed around his arm. He could feel the sticky pink saliva burning his flesh as the teeth dug deeper. The night sky and roof suddenly switched places as Travis pin-wheeled through the air. The monster was toying with him.

Just a few seconds, Squirrel only needed a few seconds to concentrate. This monster was bigger and meaner than the others, but worse yet, it seemed smarter. An image formed in Squirrel's mind and he forced it outward, spread it through his body.

A tiny silver dot welled on Squirrel's arm like a mercurial bead of sweat. Another followed and then countless others, all joining together until Squirrel's skin shimmered in the errant rays of moonlight.

Squirrel rushed forward, his steps silent, somehow muted by the material coating his skin. He launched himself towards the monster. It spun, snapping its massive jaws closed around the boy.

Pressure. That was all Squirrel felt. No pain, no panic, just a squeezing of his ribs. One or two popped, but were immediately knitted back together. Squirrel thrashed in the monster's jaws until he could get his hands near its eyes. The material rippled and leaked into the monster's eyes causing it to drop its prey.

The creature stumbled backwards, wildly shaking its head. Strings of quicksilver hung from Squirrel's hands, a metallic spider web attached to the monster. The thin threads suddenly snapped taut and the creature yowled in agony.

"Easy," Squirrel said softly. "Just relax, big fella." The monster's front legs buckled and it knelt before Squirrel. He had driven the silvery material deep into the monster's brain and now had control. Squirrel walked slowly forward, the glittering threads still connecting him to the creature, and climbed onto its muscled back.

"Great," Travis winced as he tied a section of his jacket sleeve around his arm. "So now you have a freaky cow monster to ride, but we're still running out of organic food. The slime will come for us soon. What now?"

"Now?" Squirrel, now completely coated in silver, smiled sadly. "Now we serve Andy the main course."

Travis lunged for Squirrel, trying to pull him from the back of the monster, but it was too late. The boy snapped his heels and launched the living nightmare from the roof, plunging it into the burbling mass of slime.

-46-

An entire life of fast food had filled Andy's body with pink slime, had created within him the perfect environment for the slime to incubate. Andy's body was a swirling soup of chemicals, hormones and genetically modified crap – everything that the slime thrived upon. Squirrel's body was the exact opposite.

Squirrel had always seen his parents as overzealous, albeit well intentioned. They had denied him the usual adolescent junk food and insisted that he eat only things that had words like 'free range', 'non-gmo' or 'organic' as the first part of the label. By the time Squirrel had become a young man, he had lost interest in eating the crap he saw poisoning his best friend Andy and for lack of other options had clung to the habits instilled within him by his crunchy granola parents. Squirrel's body was built with organic blocks and that was exactly what he was counting on.

The slime dissolved the cow monster soon after Squirrel dove into it, but could do nothing to the quicksilver armor that coated his skin. Squirrel kicked and pulled, swimming deeper into the goo. Andy was in here near the middle and Squirrel was going to find him.

We need to kill him, Andy. We need to kill him now!

"I'm trying!" Andy yelled, but with Squirrel actually in the slime and impervious to its effects, there was little he could do. "I can't do anything to him!"

KILL HIM! KILL HIM NOW!

Andy's inner chorus had changed from its cool, calm voice to a discordant mix of hysterics. Andy could feel the slime's panic, could hear it shrieking in his head.

"I can't do ANYTHING!" Andy screamed. "I can't – oh shit." Andy's words trailed off as he came face to silvery face with his former best friend.

"It's over, Andy," Squirrel said. "Please stop."

"I can't, Squirrel," Andy said. His words were sad and heavy. Some small piece of Andy regretted what he had become, what he had done, but he had passed the tipping point long ago. There was no turning back. "Squirrel, I'm sorry, man, but I can't stop. It's too late."

"I know," Squirrel nodded. Even though his eyes were painted in a thick layer of silver Andy could see the sadness in them.

"Squirrel, what are you doing, man?" Andy asked. His friend smiled, a long sad smile that said everything that needed to be said.

The quicksilver coating on Squirrel's body shimmered, rippling before beginning to leak off his limbs. The exposed skin sizzled and melted as the slime ate into Squirrel's body.

Andy watched as the slime he had helped create and feed dissolved his best friend. Squirrel's head was flung backwards as a garbled howl of agony escaped his exposed jaws in a spiraling trail of frothy pink bubbles. A single mercurial tear slipped down Squirrel's cheek before both it and the skin covering his face disappeared. His bones and meat sank deeper into the slime, trailing what looked like black curls of smoke.

The thick black tendrils wound through the slime, darkening the pink goo. Sections began to harden and crumble. The slime screamed in Andy's head, but even that was losing its strength. The morbid throne beneath Andy shuddered and fell away. He found himself slipping through the ooze, only to hit a hard blackened patch of dead slime, crash through it and continue downward.

Andy hit the ground with a heavy *thud!* A few seconds later, something crashed down on top of him.

"OUCH!" Andy groaned as he shifted Cece onto the ground next to him. "Are you okay?"

"Are you seriously asking me that question," Cece snapped.

"Yeah," Andy shrugged. "I can kind of see your point. Sorry."

Cece opened her mouth to yell at Andy, but seeing the sadness on his face, chose to remain silent. Large black flakes fluttered down around them like snow.

"How'd this happen?" she asked.

"Squirrel," Andy began but his voice hitched and tears rolled down his face, tracing jagged lines through the sooty black ash that caked his face. "He, uh…Squirrel he let the slime…" Cece nodded.

"Looks like Christmas in Hell," Cece said dryly as she brushed some the flakes from her hair.

Epilogue

"You hungry?" Andy asked as he opened the car door for Cece. Following the slime incident, Travis relocated both to a new town. The government wanted the mess cleaned up, but still had to cover up why an entire town, excluding one dingy health food store, had vanished in a single night. The cornerstone of that cover up was ensuring that the few remaining survivors were relocated to towns far away from each other and provided heavily padded bank accounts.

After an appeal from Travis, the agency had relented and allowed Andy and Cece to stay together. They had no family and posed no real threat. And strangely enough, after a period of adjustment and anger, the slime had brought them closer together.

With a new life and Cece at his side, Andy found the motivation he needed to reclaim his life. Squirrel had died to save him and Andy wasn't going to squander his second chance. He ate right, worked out and avoided fast food restaurants like the plague.

"I'm always hungry lately," Cece smiled from the passenger's seat. "I better watch myself. I'm starting to get a little pooch." She playfully patted her stomach. Somewhere deep inside Cece's stomach something small and pink stirred. Something hungry and demanding.

"You want to hit up that salad place?" Andy started the car.

"I don't know," Cece shrugged. "I think I could really go for a cheeseburger."

Acknowledgements

To Gary and the rest of Severed Press, I thank you for taking a chance on a horror story about aliens, cheeseburgers and pink slime. The creative freedom is much appreciated.

As always, I need to thank my family and friends. Your support continues to be the cornerstone of my foundation. I know that the things I learned and shared while researching *Pink Slime* were not always the most appetizing. Thanks for putting up with me and sorry if I ruined ground beef for any of you.

Finally, to all the readers who take the time to read and/or review my ramblings, I whole-heartedly thank you! Please feel free to find me on Facebook or Twitter.

www.ingramcontent.com/pod-product-compliance
Lightning Source LLC
Chambersburg PA
CBHW050743230626
47052CB00004BA/1099